PUFFIN BOOKS
THE MAGIC OF THE LOST EARRINGS

Sudha Murty was born in 1950 in Shiggaon, in north Karnataka. She did her MTech in computer science. A philanthropist, a teacher and an author, she is the chairperson of Murty Foundation. She is also a member of the Rajya Sabha. A prolific writer in English and Kannada, she has written novels, technical books, travelogues, collections of short stories and non-fictional pieces, and several bestselling titles for children. Her books have been translated into all the major Indian languages. Sudha Murty is the recipient of the R.K. Narayan Award for Literature. She received the Padma Shri in 2006, the Attimabbe Award from the Government of Karnataka for excellence in Kannada literature in 2011, the Lifetime Achievement Award at the 2018 Crossword Book Awards and the Padma Bhushan in 2023. She has also received twenty honorary doctorates. She weaves magical tales and especially enjoys writing for young readers. A generation of children has grown up reading her books, and her stories have been included in textbooks across schools in India. To read more about her books, please visit www.sudhamurty.in.

ALSO IN PUFFIN BY SUDHA MURTY

How the Sea Became Salty
How the Onion Got Its Layers
How the Mango Got Its Magic
How the Earth Got Its Beauty
How the Bamboo Got Its Bounty
How to be Happy with Who You Are
How I Taught My Grandmother to Read and Other Stories
The Magic Drum and Other Favourite Stories
Grandma's Bag of Stories
Grandparents' Bag of Stories
Grandpa's Bag of Stories
The Bird with Golden Wings
The Magic of the Lost Temple
The Magic of the Lost Story
The Serpent's Revenge: Unusual Tales from the Mahabharata
The Man from the Egg: Unusual Tales about the Trinity
The Upside-Down King: Unusual Tales about Rama and Krishna
The Daughter from a Wishing Tree: Unusual Tales about Women in Mythology
The Sage with Two Horns: Unusual Tales from Mythology
The Sudha Murty Children's Treasury
Unusual Tales from Indian Mythology

The Magic of the Lost Earrings

SUDHA MURTY
Illustrations by David Yambem

PUFFIN BOOKS
An imprint of Penguin Random House

PUFFIN BOOKS

Puffin Books is an imprint of the Penguin Random House group of companies whose addresses can be found at global.penguinrandomhouse.com

Published by Penguin Random House India Pvt. Ltd
4th Floor, Capital Tower 1, MG Road,
Gurugram 122 002, Haryana, India

First published in Puffin Books by Penguin Random House India 2025

Text copyright © Sudha Murty 2025
Illustrations copyright © David Yambem 2025

All rights reserved

10 9 8 7 6 5 4 3 2 1

This is a work of fiction. Unless otherwise indicated, all the names, characters, events described in this book are either the product of the author's imagination or used in a fictitious manner. Any resemblance to actual persons, living or dead, or actual events is purely coincidental. Certain long-standing institutions and geographical locations are mentioned, but the characters involved are wholly imaginary.

All sketches in the book are the perception of the author specifically created for explaining her views, and the use thereof shall remain limited to interpreting the author's views in this book. The image features depicted therein, whether historical and contemporary, are neither purported to be correct nor authentic.

Please note that no part of this book may be used or reproduced in any manner for the purpose of training artificial intelligence technologies or systems.

ISBN 9780143479802

Book design and layout by Samar Bansal

Typeset in Cochin LT Pro by Manipal Technologies Limited, Manipal
Printed at Thomson Press India Ltd, New Delhi

This book is sold subject to the condition that it shall not, by way of trade or otherwise, be lent, resold, hired out or otherwise circulated without the publisher's prior consent in any form of binding or cover other than that in which it is published and without a similar condition including this condition being imposed on the subsequent purchaser.

www.penguin.co.in

*To Usha and Yashvir Sunak and their
families — uprooted twice from their homeland,
with deep admiration for their resilience
in making new countries their own . . .*

Kittu, Nooni and Ajji

Contents

Author's Note ix

Holiday Plans 1
A Mysterious Discovery in Ujjain 9
Wonders of Amritsar 23
The First Clue 34
The Next Piece of the Puzzle 49
Delhi Adventures 62
London Calling 84
Exploring and Discovering 97
Threads of the Past 111
The Magic of the Lost Earrings 122
Full Circle 141

Author's Note

Before 1947, India's map included regions that are today Pakistan and Bangladesh. For those of us born in independent India, it's difficult to grasp what it means for a country to be divided—how a land, a people and a culture, can be split apart by lines drawn on paper. Borders, we often forget, are not permanent. They shift with time, shaped by political decisions and historical forces.

Imagine being told that the land your family has lived on for generations, where your ancestors lived and where your language was shaped, and your customs were born—no longer belongs to you. This was the lived reality for millions during the Partition of India. The trauma they experienced, the resilience they had to develop, and the hope they needed to seek a better future are experiences that define the immigrant story.

This book is dedicated to Yashvir and Usha Sunak, who represent many others who endured these very hardships. Forced to leave Gujranwala and Abbottabad in Pakistan after Partition, they rebuilt their lives in Nairobi and Dar es Salaam. And then, once again, they had to leave everything behind and move to England, carrying nothing but immense hope.

This was not their choice. History chose that for them. Not by choice, they had to leave behind lives they had carefully built, stepping into foreign lands with nothing but resilience and hope. I hold deep admiration for such individuals—those who, despite unimaginable challenges, integrated themselves into new societies and made valuable contributions wherever they lived. Their journeys are a testament to the human spirit.

I believe that understanding our history is essential. Because without knowing our history, we cannot truly understand who we are or where we are going. These lessons must go beyond the classroom; they should live in everyday life and in the stories we tell.

The Magic of the Lost Earrings

The Magic of the Lost Earrings is the third book in the Nooni series. Nooni's compassion, dedication and courage to help others should serve as an inspiration to our children.

I hope our young people learn the importance of hard work, courage, resilience and a love for their country and fellow citizens. These qualities, after all, matter far more than medals or accolades. They are the quiet, enduring strengths that hold our shared humanity together.

This is my fiftieth book. The first book I ever wrote was in 1979 in Kannada—my mother tongue. There weren't many publishers at the time, so it was published only in 1981. Since then, I've written eighteen books in Kannada and thirty-two in English. My work has been translated into thirteen or fourteen Indian languages, and across formats, there are now over 300 titles.

I am deeply grateful to my readers of all ages. Their feedback, enthusiasm, and affection continue to encourage me to keep writing!

My sincere gratitude to the team at Penguin Random House India, who have brought out the majority of my books—for both children and adults.

My heartfelt thanks to my long-time publisher, Sohini Mitra; my bright, young and enthusiastic editor, Simran Kaur; and David Yambem for his wonderful illustrations.

Sudha Murty
10 May 2025
Bangalore

Holiday Plans

It was the end of January and the last phase of winter in Bangalore. The city had lost its old title as a Pensioners' Paradise and was now better known as the Silicon Valley of India—famous for its technology and traffic jams.

Nooni was extremely happy that morning. There were two reasons. First, her school would be closing from 10 to 20 February for ten days. This was because they were hosting the All-India Teachers' Conference on campus. The principal had sent a letter to all parents explaining the situation and assuring them that the next academic year would begin ten days early to make up for it.

The second reason for Nooni's joy was her dance. She had been learning Kuchipudi, and her troupe had been selected to perform in London as part of Vasant Utsava: A Celebration of Spring. The cultural department was organizing the event at the Bharatiya Vidya Bhavan (BVB), and the dance group would be travelling in April and May to showcase India's rich heritage.

Excited, Nooni called her grandparents to share the news. Over the last few years, she had grown very close to them. Ajji picked up the phone.

'Nooni, I was about to call you with some wonderful news,' she said. 'Ajja and I have decided to travel to north India. It's something we have wanted to do for a long time. We have also decided to visit Radha in London this summer, since she has been inviting us for years. Radha was Ajja's only niece, settled in London for the last twenty-five years.

Nooni jumped with joy and said, 'What a coincidence! I have an unexpected break of ten days. I would love to join you for the north India trip! I want to see Delhi.'

Since the speaker was on, Ajja's voice rang out, 'I want to visit Amritsar and the Wagah Border!'

Nooni could hear him clearly.

'And I want to see Ujjain,' said Ajji.

'Let's plan in such a way that we can visit all three places in ten days. We will talk to your parents.'

'Why Ujjain, Ajji?' asked Nooni.

'That I'll explain on the trip,' said Ajji. 'It holds an important place in Indian history and culture.'

'Now that you are older, you can start making reservations online. We are not good at all that,' said Ajja, smiling at Ajji.

'Please book the tickets and look for economical but clean and safe hotels. To go around, also book the taxi service from the hotel. Nooni, you are the leader on this tour and, for a change, we will be your followers.'

Nooni beamed. 'Ajji, sometimes allow me to speak too!' she said playfully. 'Please adjust your London trip dates so we can enjoy Vasant Utsava together.'

'What is Vasant Utsava?' asked Ajja.

'It's an ancient festival, going back over 2,500 years. It was documented in *Indica*, a book written by Megasthenes, a Greek historian at the time of Chandragupta Maurya. The dancers don't wear regular jewellery, but ornaments made of flowers. They dress in bright colours to celebrate spring. The great poet Amir Khusrau composed the song "Sakal Ban". It's a famous poem celebrating the arrival of spring,' Ajji replied.

Ajja chuckled.

'You never miss a chance to turn into a history teacher!'

'If we don't know our history, we're bound to repeat its mistakes,' Ajji said.

Nooni laughed. She always enjoyed her grandparents' playful banter.

Soon, Ajja and Ajji arrived in Bangalore, and together they planned the trip meticulously.

Nooni, now fifteen, was proud to take the lead. She was comfortable with the latest apps for online payments and bookings, maps, and more. She excitedly made their travel plans.

Their first stop was Indore, where Nooni's maternal grandparents lived. But they were away on a group tour of south India, enjoying the pleasant weather. Since Nooni's plans were made at the last minute, it wasn't possible to change theirs. It would have been a hassle to stay in their house in their absence, and since all three had visited Indore before, they decided to skip it.

Instead, they booked a taxi directly from Indore airport to Ujjain. They would stay in Ujjain for the night and head back to the Indore airport the very next day. Their next stop would be Amritsar, followed by Delhi, and then back to Bangalore by flight. Everything had been well planned for the ten-day trip.

Nooni's maternal grandmother helped them book a reliable taxi service in Indore.

Before leaving, her parents sat her down.

'Nooni, don't get carried away just because you're good with technology. Be patient with Ajja and Ajji. They are older and might need time to do things. Let them go at their own pace. I will tell them not to carry much cash. You can make all the payments online. Don't shop too much or increase your luggage. Most of all, enjoy their company and discover new places,' said Usha.

Nooni nodded. She agreed to everything immediately.

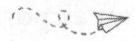

On the day of travel, the three of them arrived at Bangalore's Terminal 2. It was Ajja and Ajji's first time flying from this terminal. They were surprised to see the expanse and decor of this terminal.

Ajja, who was easily impressed, said, 'This is wonderful! People from around the world can see our airports are on par with the best. I am very proud of the progress my country has made.'

Ajji smiled but didn't comment.

Nooni knew that Ajji was not easily impressed. She was logical, practical and curious. As Ajji had been a history teacher for a long time, she always asked questions—why things were a certain way. Perhaps that's why her stories always felt so vivid and convincing.

Ajji said, 'This is indeed beautiful. But maintaining this green space and cane structures is a difficult task and equally important.'

After check-in, they got their boarding passes and moved to security. The plane was delayed a bit. While Ajji and Nooni waited at the gate, Ajja wandered off, admiring the architecture and design of the airport.

'Ajji, tell me, why do you want to go to Ujjain? It doesn't even have an airport! It is so difficult to reach there.'

'Ujjain holds a special place in Indian history. It has been my dream to visit Ujjain since I was a teenager. When I was studying Sanskrit, I always admired Kalidasa—India's greatest poet. He was from Ujjain. He described the river Shipra, the temple of Mahakal, the streets of Ujjain and the kingdom of Avanti in his literary works.'

'So that is why you want to visit Ujjain?'

'That's only one reason. I'll tell you more once we're there.'

'What is this Mahakal Temple, Ajji? Why is it so famous?' asked Nooni.

'Mahakal means Shiva, the Lord of Time. The temple is called that because Ujjain once served as India's prime meridian, just like Greenwich in England today. That's also why an observatory, called the Jantar Mantar or Vedha Shala, was built there by Maharaja Sawai Jai Singh II.

'I read that Krishna studied near Ujjain. Is that true, Ajji?' asked Nooni.

'Yes. It is believed that Lord Krishna, Balarama, and their friend Sudama studied at Sandipani Ashram near Ujjain. It is said to be a famous *gurukul*,' Ajji explained.

By then, the boarding call had been announced, and the three of them boarded the plane, ready for the next chapter in their adventure.

A Mysterious Discovery in Ujjain

At Indore airport, a taxi was waiting for them. Nooni took the lead and got into the car.

'Ajji, do you know that Indore is the cleanest city in India? It has won the national cleanliness award seven times in a row!'

Ajja and Ajji looked around and saw that the city truly was very clean.

Nooni continued, 'It's because the city has a well-planned waste segregation, conversion and disposal system.'

Ajja nodded. 'Yes, I've read about it. To maintain a clean city like this, both the public and the municipal corporation must work together and take responsibility. Only then is it possible.

I've also heard that this city is famous for its wide variety of food. Sarafa Bazaar and Chappan Dukan are especially well-known. And they're no-vehicle areas, too.'

Ajja had clearly done his research well.

Nooni said, 'When I visited last time, I had dal pakwan.'

'Is pakwan sweet?' asked Ajji.

'No, it's a kind of savoury dish,' replied Nooni. 'It's a Sindhi dish. If time permits, we should definitely try it.'

'Yes. People from the Sindh area are called Sindhis. After the Partition, many of them came to India. They settled in cities like Pune, Indore, Jaipur and Chennai. They brought their rich culinary traditions. Dishes like dal kadi and dal pakwan are some of their specialities. They also have a distinctive embroidery style known as the Sindhi stitch,' replied Ajja.

'When I think of Indore, I think of Rani Ahilya Bai Holkar,' said Ajji. 'She was a young widow, a generous queen, a skilled warrior and a great philanthropist—a rare combination. Ahilya Bai changed the destiny of her people. She travelled across India and restored temples at Badrinath, Kedarnath, Kathmandu, Varanasi, Haridwar and many other places. She also helped establish the art of weaving the famous Maheshwari saris,'

Nooni felt that Ajji was getting emotional.

The car was headed towards Ujjain.

Ajja, being a farmer, was curious to see the crops growing all around. 'Just look at this land and the crops,' he said, eyes shining. 'So green and fertile! You could grow almost anything here.'

Ajji nodded with a smile. 'This region is called Malwa. It's always been prized by kings and rulers for its rich soil and bountiful harvests.'

Nooni soaked in the beautiful landscapes with her grandparents.

After about two hours, they reached Ujjain and checked into the hotel. They ate a light lunch with the driver who was also their guide and then left for a city tour.

'Let's first go to see the Shipra River,' Ajji said.

'She is very sacred, and once every twelve years the Kumbh Mela is held here,' the driver replied.

Nooni, who had been listening intently, leaned forward from the back seat. 'When is the next Kumbh Mela?' she asked, her eyes wide with curiosity.

The driver replied, 'The Simhastha Kumbh Mela is in 2028.'

As the car rolled along the road by the river, Ajji looked out thoughtfully at the landscape and asked, 'Where are the caves of Bhartrihari?'

'They are across the Shipra River,' the driver said as he pointed at the river. 'The great philosopher and scholar who ruled this area is remembered by very few people. I am impressed that you know about him,' the driver smiled.

Ajji chuckled softly. 'When I was in school, we were taught a few *shlokas* from Bhartrihari Nitishataka. That's how I came to know about him.'

The driver nodded. The car then slowed a little as they approached a temple complex, and he gestured towards it.

'There are many interesting places and well-known figures connected to Ujjain. For example, the Avantika Temple, where Goddess Avantika was worshipped by King Vikramaditya, attracts thousands of pilgrims. The famous princess Vasavadatta is a well-known name in literature. And Harsiddhi Mata is one of the oldest *shakti peetha* (holy shrine) here—it's believed that whatever you wish for at this shrine will be granted. That's why she is called Harsiddhi. Ujjain was also the capital of King Vikramaditya during the Gupta period. You'd need a couple of days to see everything properly.'

After taking a walk around, all of them went to the Mahakal Temple, Sandipani Ashram and the shrine of Harsiddhi Mata where they performed a small puja.

By then, the sun had begun to dip lower in the sky, casting a golden glow over the city. They returned to the hotel at night after watching the *aarti* at the Shipra Ghats and again at the Mahakal Temple.

It had been a long and full day—starting with their journey from Bangalore to Indore and then onwards to Ujjain. Though Ajja and Ajji were tired, they were deeply satisfied.

The next morning, Ajji turned to Nooni as they packed up. 'Nooni, let's rearrange your luggage and backpack. Yesterday, wherever I got the *kumkum* and other *prasad*, I put them in the front pocket of your backpack. Please take all that out—we'll put it in a separate cover. I will carry the prasad and share it with people in our village who can't travel so far. They'll be happy to receive it.'

Nooni nodded and began emptying her bag. As she unzipped the outer pocket—the one meant for coins—she felt it was unusually heavy. She paused

and asked Ajji if she had put anything in there. Ajji said she had not.

Curious, Nooni unzipped the coin pocket and found a small red velvet purse inside. She had never seen it before.

'Is this your purse?' she asked, holding it up for Ajji to see.

'No, neither is it mine nor have I seen it before,' Ajji said, a little surprised.

Ajja, who had been reading the newspaper nearby, overheard the conversation and walked over to find out what they were talking about.

Nooni held out the little pouch. It was a beautiful, soft red pouch. She then unzipped it. Inside, wrapped in white parchment paper, was a pair of shiny gold earrings. The design was intricate—each shaped like a peacock with green emeralds studded across its feathers and a tiny ruby for the eye.

Of course, one could easily tell that it was a very old design and not a modern one. The earrings looked valuable.

Nooni turned the earrings over carefully. Something was engraved on the back, but it wasn't in English or Hindi. In fact, she had never seen such letters before.

Ajji was worried and asked, 'Who could have kept it in your bag?'

Ajja said, 'Has someone purposely kept it in your bag? Let's check the pouch again. Is there something else in it too?'

Nooni opened the pouch again and felt around the inside carefully. She then pulled out a small piece of pink paper which was folded. She unfolded it and read:

Dear Bubbly,

Happy sixteenth birthday. This is my gift to you. These earrings have a long history and are very precious and rare. I have saved them for a long time. Please enjoy wearing them, and I hope you pass them on to your next generation...

With affection,
Dadi

'This doesn't give us any clue about whom it belongs to. It just says that it is a gift from a grandmother to her granddaughter,' said Ajja, as he shook his head.

'It looks like it is made of real gold and precious stones,' Ajji said, looking closely at the earrings again.

She turned to Nooni. 'But how did this end up in your bag? We should retrace our steps. Maybe that will give us a clue.'

Nooni nodded and sat down to think. She went over their journey in her head—arriving at the airport, checking in their luggage, waiting at the gate, and so on. But the backpack had always been on her shoulder.

Suddenly she remembered. 'Ajji, do you recall that when Ajja was admiring the airport's interiors, you and I went to the washroom? I gave you my backpack to hold.'

Ajji nodded and began recalling each of their actions in detail. Nooni had handed her the bag just outside the restroom. While washing her hands, Ajji had placed the backpack near the basin. Then, worried it might get wet, she had kept it on the baggage rack nearby. After cleaning her spectacles and drying them, she picked up the bag and returned it to Nooni, who slipped it on her shoulder.

'Then we went through security and stopped at the bookstore,' Nooni added. 'I kept my bag on a table and bent down to search the children's section. Then I went to another section and picked up a sudoku book. I came back and pushed the book into my bag as Ajja paid for it.'

'Even on the flight,' Nooni went on, 'I placed our bags in the overhead bin myself—first my backpack, then Ajji's handbag, followed by Ajja's crossbody bag. It would've been really hard for someone to unzip just the coin pocket and place something so carefully inside without being noticed.'

'So, the only possibility would be either in the restroom when Ajji cleaned her spectacles, or at the bookstore,' Nooni replied thoughtfully.

But Ajji could not remember anyone coming and doing all this, as there had been many other items in the baggage rack, and it was rush hour as well.

Ajji felt very sorry for the lady who had lost the earrings.

Nooni, meanwhile, had held the earrings near her ears and was looking into a mirror, curious to see how she looked while wearing the earrings.

With a stern voice, Ajji said, 'Nooni, please don't do that. I know you love jewellery because of your dance performances, but these don't belong to us. We will try to get this to its rightful owner at the earliest.'

'No, Ajji,' Nooni said quickly, lowering the earrings. 'I didn't mean to keep them. I was just looking at how beautiful they are. I promise I will definitely help you trace the owner.'

'I agree with you,' said Ajja. 'It's likely someone accidentally mixed up their bag with Nooni's and placed the pouch in hers by mistake—maybe during all the bustle in the restroom or at the bookstore, where she left the backpack unattended.'

They turned their attention back to the velvet pouch. Embroidered in gold thread on the front were the words: *Khurana Jewellers, Near Harmandir Sahib, Bhanumati Road, Amritsar.*

'Here, at least we found some clue,' said Ajja.

'Yes, Ajja. The pouch itself is so beautiful. When we go to the jewellers, I will gift one to Ajji to keep her jewellery,' said Nooni.

'Ajji doesn't have so much jewellery to keep in a pouch!' Ajja said with a chuckle.

'She has spent all her money building her library with so many books,' he added teasingly.

Ajji immediately responded, 'Of course, that is the real jewel.'

Nooni laughed. She had always felt that Ajji was smarter and wittier than Ajja, whereas Ajja was more patient. That was why she always enjoyed their company. What she admired most was how they were always eager to learn, no matter their age. It was a gift to have such grandparents.

Thus, the new adventure of finding the rightful owner of the beautiful lost earrings began in Ujjain.

Wonders of Amritsar

The next morning, while they were travelling towards Indore airport, Nooni said, 'Shall we inform the Terminal 2 airport authorities in Bangalore? Maybe the earrings ended up in the airport's lost and found.'

'We can. I will call your father and ask him to check with the airport authorities,' said Ajja. 'In the meantime, since the pouch has an address from Amritsar, and we are headed there anyway, we might as well check in Amritsar. If we go to that shop, they might be able to help us.'

All of them agreed.

Unlike Bangalore, Indore airport was a modest one. There were many shops exhibiting and selling tribal art, Maheshwari and Chanderi saris, block-printed bedsheets, kurta sets and many more items and artefacts.

'Madhya Pradesh is one of the most culturally rich states with its tribal communities, unique weaving traditions, folk music and instruments. There's so much to see here that it is said one can't see it all in just one visit. One must come at least four times!' Ajji said.

Nooni's eyes widened. 'Four times?'

'Yes! One trip for the Gwalior side, which includes the Gwalior Fort, Badavalai Mitavali and Bateswar temples. Another for Jabalpur and the marble rocks through which the Narmada flows. Then the capital, Bhopal, with the Ashokan Sanchi Stupa, Vidisha and more places nearby. And finally, places like Ujjain, Indore, Mandu and Pachmarhi.'

'Yes,' Ajja pitched in. 'It is one of the few states with no coastline—landlocked from all sides. The lifeline is River Narmada, one of only two major Indian rivers that flow westwards. All the others flow east. It eventually joins the Arabian Sea.'

Nooni was impressed. 'Ajja, your general knowledge is too good,' she said.

'I read every day, Nooni. It keeps my mind fresh and active,' said Ajja.

Soon, they reached Amritsar—a city alive with colours, aromas and energy. The streets were lined with old and new shops, innumerable eateries, many small and big gurdwaras. The shops were full of woollen wear, pashmina shawls, embroidered dupattas, phulkari and Bagh-print textiles.

Shortly after they checked into the hotel room, Ajji said, 'Let's not have a regular lunch. Let's explore the city and taste some authentic local dishes. Punjab is famous for its iconic dishes like Amritsari kulcha, pindi chole, among others.'

Ajja and Nooni agreed. The moonlight mingled with the golden glow of shop lights, giving the streets an illuminated look.

They chose a lively eatery tucked into one corner of the bazaar. The owner greeted them warmly. They all responded and sat at a table.

He handed them a menu and said, 'We recommend you try out our Punjabi food, which is unique. You will not get anything like this anywhere else. You must try our makki-di-roti with sarson-ka-saag. You can start with pista lassi or malai lassi. You can even try our chola bhatura, for which Punjab is famous. We also serve delicious parathas with aloo, gobi and mixed vegetable stuffings.'

Before anyone could answer, he went to the next question.

'If you come to Punjab and don't eat paneer, you will regret it all your life. Do you want to eat paneer pakoda, paneer paratha or paneer tikki?' he went on.

Ajja smiled politely and interrupted, 'We prefer food that's not too oily. Could we try some grilled vegetables, please?'

'Oh yes, I have my own tandoor. Whatever vegetables you want, I can grill them.'

'Can I see the tandoor?' Nooni was curious.

The owner eagerly took her to a corner where a large clay oven stood.

'This is a tandoor—a cylindrical mud oven. Traditionally, it uses coal or wood. I use both gas and coal depending on what's available. Some places even use electric tandoors nowadays.'

Nooni could see stacks of rotis kept around the tandoor.

When their food arrived, the generous portions took them by surprise. Hot parathas, soft kulchas and a colourful array of grilled vegetables were served. All of them thoroughly enjoyed the food.

Nooni paid the bill online, including the tip. Her grandparents felt proud that their granddaughter was growing up so quickly—confident, independent and tech-savvy.

Back at the hotel, before hitting the bed, Nooni explained the itinerary to her grandparents, 'Ajja, Ajji, we will go and see Harmandir Sahib and the jeweller in the morning. In the evening, we will visit the Wagah border. After that, we can explore the city a bit more and leave for Delhi.'

Ajja and Ajji agreed.

After a bath and a hearty breakfast, they set off that morning to visit Harmandir Sahib, famously known as the Golden Temple.

On their way to the gurdwara, Ajji explained, 'The gurdwara sits in the middle of a man-made pool called the Amrit Sarovar. The gurdwara was destroyed and rebuilt several times, but Maharaja

Ranjit Singh finally made it what we see today. He even had the inner sanctum plated in gold.'

Ajja added, 'Sikhism puts a lot of emphasis on *seva* — selfless service. Therefore, you will see people cleaning, cooking, managing footwear and even polishing steps. Everywhere in the world, every gurdwara offers *langar*, a free community meal. People from all faiths are welcome.'

When the trio reached the gurdwara, they saw many devotees. All visitors removed their shoes and walked through the shallow water canals meant to cleanse the feet before entering the holy space. Everyone walked barefoot along marble corridors with their heads covered. Ajji used her *pallu*, Nooni tied a scarf, and Ajja collected a head cover from a nearby counter. Though there were many devotees, all the areas were spotlessly clean.

They entered the gurdwara and saw the Guru Granth Sahib (holy book) in the middle of the sanctum sanctorum. A few groups of devotees sat cross-legged on the floor, their eyes closed, hands folded in prayer. A group of musicians sat with traditional instruments, singing hymns in soothing, rhythmic tones. Ajji whispered to Nooni, 'This is called kirtan.'

The three of them quietly walked around the sanctum, bowed down to the Granth Sahib and came out. Before leaving the premises, they ate prasad.

'Let's go to the jeweller and finish our work,' said Nooni. She knew that the shop was close by.

When they reached the shop, they were informed that due to some unexpected electrical repair, the shop would reopen only the following morning.

'Let's go back and have lunch at the gurdwara itself,' Ajja said.

'Not lunch. It's called langar,' Ajji reminded him.

Nooni was very excited to have langar at Harmandir Sahib.

At the langar hall, people sat on mats in long rows. Those who could not sit down were offered chairs and tables. Volunteers moved swiftly and humbly along the rows, serving food to all. Roti, dal, sabzi, rice, raita and a sweet dish were served on steel *thalis*. The rotis were warm and soft, and the aroma of the food was inviting. All three of them sat cross-legged on the floor and ate with gratitude.

After lunch, they joined a tourist bus headed for Wagah, a village on the India–Pakistan border. 'Typically, every evening, a parade is held at the border. On the Indian side, it is conducted by the Border Security Force (BSF), and on the Pakistani side, it is conducted by the Pakistan Rangers,' Ajja told Nooni while they were on their way.

The crowds on both sides of the border were enthusiastic and spirited, waving flags and cheering.

Dressed in ceremonial uniforms, soldiers from both sides performed their high-energy drills with synchronized steps. They marched up to the gate, saluted their flags and conducted the ritual lowering of the national flags. This drill is followed every day, irrespective of the season, at sunset.

Nooni, Ajja and Ajji went early with the other tourists and booked their seats.

'We must respect the people in uniform because they take care of our safety so that we all can live in harmony in a democratic country,' Ajja said.

After the drill, they all returned to their hotel and slept after a quick dinner.

The First Clue

The next morning, they visited the Partition Museum. Located in the historic Town Hall of Amritsar, the museum, which opened in 2017, is the first of its kind in the world. Once a British headquarters and jail, the red-brick colonial building now tells the story of one of the most painful chapters in South Asian history.

The Partition of India was one of the most defining moments in the nation's history. It was perhaps the largest migration in human history, with nearly twenty million affected. The museum captured the trauma, grief and resilience of millions affected by the Partition of 1947. Photographs, letters, recordings, and artefacts brought the experiences of displaced Sindhi and Punjabi families to life. It reminded visitors that

behind every political decision were countless personal tragedies.

Nooni became still and said, 'Ajja, now I understand what it means to be safe. How lucky we are. We are in the same country, the same state, speaking the same language and having most of our relatives nearby.'

Their hearts were heavy with sadness.

That afternoon, they returned to Khurana Jewellers. It was a big building and had two or three sections. When they went in, the staff greeted them and offered coffee, tea, lassi, cold drinks, and so on. Another female staff member handed them the catalogue and asked politely, 'What would you like to see? Punjab is famous for heavy *kundan* work. We have Lahori designs, which are famous for intricate work.'

Nooni gently interrupted, 'We haven't come here to shop. We are here to make an enquiry and would like to meet the manager.'

She nodded and directed them to the fourth floor.

On the fourth floor, they entered a stylish, modestly furnished office. There were two men,

one middle-aged and the other a little older. When they saw Nooni and her grandparents, they greeted them.

Nooni quickly opened her bag and showed them the pouch.

They immediately recognized it and one of them said, 'Yes, the pouch is from our shop. It's one of our newer designs—we began using it just last year.'

Ajji opened the pouch, took the earrings in her hand, and asked, 'Do you recognize these earrings?'

The younger man said, 'Oh yes, I do, because they are unusually different and antique.' He turned it around.

'Do you see the letters engraved here on the back? That's the Gurmukhi script. Are you interested in selling them?'

'No,' Ajji replied. 'We are trying to return them to their rightful owner. Do you remember who brought them in?'

'Yes. It is a special design, which makes it quite easily recognizable. About a week ago, an elderly woman came here and gave this pair for polishing. She seemed sad and said she had once owned another identical pair with red stones but had sold them long ago in Amritsar. While we were polishing this pair, she went to Harmandir Sahib to pray. When she came back, she paid, collected the pouch and left.'

'Would you have her name or contact details?' Nooni asked, hopeful.

He shook his head. 'Unfortunately, no. We only collect personal details when items are bought or sold—not for services like polishing.'

Nooni's face fell.

She looked at Ajja and Ajji and did not know what to do. They had hoped this would lead somewhere. But nothing came of it. It was like searching for a needle in a haystack.

'It's a beautiful pair,' the younger man said, carefully returning the earrings. 'You don't see craftsmanship like this any more. It is an antique.'

'Why do you say it is an antique piece?' Nooni asked the shop person.

'By law, any ornament over a hundred years old is considered antique. The Antiquities Act applies to such items,' said the shopkeeper.

'What about the ones that are not antique but quite old?' asked Ajji.

'Those aren't considered antiques by law. They're treated like any other piece of jewellery,' replied the shopkeeper.

There was silence.

'If I may ask, you don't know the owner of these earrings, so where did you find them, and why do you want to return them?'

'We believe this might be a family heirloom and must be very precious; hence, we would like to return them,' Ajja explained.

The older man, who had been quietly listening, finally spoke, 'I appreciate your honesty and effort. We've been in this business for five generations, always upholding ethical standards. My father had a rule: if anyone came with an antique piece to sell, we would not accept it. Instead, we sent them to antique dealers who could offer a fair value—especially before the 1977 Act changed the rules. That law, like many others, came long after the older ones introduced by Lord Curzon. I don't know if you will be successful or not, but my father had a friend, a professor of history, who collected antique jewellery as a hobby. He always paid more than the market rate. His name was Kewal Ram.'

'How do you fix a price for any antique? Isn't it priceless?' asked Ajji.

'True,' replied the elderly shopkeeper, 'but people often sell such pieces under financial duress, and many buyers melt them down without understanding their true value.'

Suddenly, Ajji remembered something. 'You said the old lady had another pair with red rubies that she had sold in this city. Is there any way to trace it through that sale?'

'Maybe,' the man said thoughtfully. 'When Partition happened in 1947, many refugees crossed the borders on both sides, and many women sold their precious ornaments for survival. Shops like ours referred them to trusted antique collectors. Kewal Ram was one of them. He often bought small items like rings and earrings. But he has since passed away. I don't know whether the other pair was bought by Kewal Ram ji or sold elsewhere. One can only guess. His grandson runs a computer business somewhere in the city.'

'Could we get his address?' Nooni asked, hope flickering again.

The man nodded appreciatively. 'Most people wouldn't bother to return something so valuable. I respect what you're doing.' He reached for an old register and jotted down an address. 'I can't guarantee his family still lives there,' he said as he handed over the paper.

The three thanked him sincerely and left.

Outside, Nooni said, 'This is the first real clue. The earrings belonged to an old lady. She had two pairs, and now we know one was sold. We are getting closer.'

The address given by the jeweller was difficult to trace. He had mentioned Chandan Cinema Hall, opposite Lovely Garden—but when they arrived, the cinema hall had been replaced by a sprawling shopping complex, and instead of the garden, there were rows of apartment buildings. They found themselves in front of a bustling mini-supermarket called Kewal Bazaar. The narrow lanes were filled with shops.

They had come with a hope that Amritsar would be their last destination, but now they stood there, clueless and uncertain.

They decided to go inside the over-decorated bazaar, which was lined with many small shops where people were engrossed in shopping.

'Let's try asking someone older. They might remember the Kewal Ram family,' Ajja suggested.

After checking a few shops, they finally spotted two elderly men talking to each other.

Nooni approached them and asked, 'Excuse me, Uncle. Do you know anything about Kewal Ram ji, who used to own a big house here?'

One of them pointed to a showroom close by and said, 'Yes, he lived here. Some of the showrooms in this bazaar belong to his family. There was also a house that belonged to Kewal Ram here. After his death, his family moved away. You could ask at that showroom; it belongs to Kewal Ram's family. Someone at the shop might know more.'

They went to the showroom, and Ajja enquired at the desk, 'Do you know anyone related to Kewal Ram?'

'I'm not sure about Kewal Ram,' the woman at the desk replied. 'But the owner here is Amrit Ram.'

'Please, could you share his contact details? We've come all the way from the south to meet him,' Ajji said.

The woman said she wasn't allowed to give out his number, but she could connect the call from the reception.

Once the line was connected, the woman explained the situation and handed over the telephone to Ajja.

'Good evening. We are looking for Kewal Ram. Did he used to live in this area?'

'Of course,' came the reply. 'He was my grandfather. But who are you?'

'We have some specific work with Kewal Ram, and we are visiting from south India. We need to speak to you in person,' said Ajja.

After a long pause, he shared his address and asked them to come to his house.

They took an auto to reach Kewal Ram's residence. The house was on the outskirts of the city—a large mansion with a sprawling garden, guarded by two security men. They were ushered into a luxurious living room, where a well-dressed man in his forties entered and introduced himself as Amrit Ram.

'Hello ji, I'm Amrit Ram. Please, have a seat.'

As they settled down on a large leather sofa, a young boy came over and arranged plates of snacks and sweets, along with glasses of cold drinks and lassi, in front of them.

'We are from Bangalore, in Karnataka. We visited Khurana Jewellers on Bhanumati Road and learnt that your grandfather had a hobby of collecting antique jewellery. We are trying to trace the owner of a pair of peacock-designed earrings studded with rubies. We were told he may have purchased a similar pair many years ago,' Ajja explained.

'We are only taking a chance to find out, and we are sorry for disturbing you. We are not here to buy. We are just regular people—my husband served briefly in the army before becoming a farmer, and I'm a retired history teacher. This is our granddaughter Anoushka. We affectionately call her Nooni,' Ajji added.

Nooni stepped forward and said, 'I accidentally received a pair of antique earrings in my backpack. We are trying to return them to the rightful owner. We discovered that the owner may have had another pair, sold perhaps several years ago. If your grandfather bought them and kept a record of the seller, we'd be incredibly grateful for that information.'

Amrit was impressed by their sincerity.

'I am not an antique dealer. It was my dada ji's hobby. He always paid double the market value and kept everything well documented. After he passed away, I inherited a collection of rings, earrings and nose pins. Over a period of time, it became risky; our house was targeted for burglary twice because word had spread that we had antiques. I'm a software engineer and run a company in Singapore. We've been fortunate, and showrooms at Kewal Bazaar are doing well too. So, I decided to donate the entire collection to the National Museum in Delhi. Everything is now government property, on display for all to see.'

'That's wonderful,' said Ajja. 'But do you have a record of the items you donated?'

'Yes, I have digitized all the details. If you describe the item, I will be able to search the database, and if there's a match, I'll show it to you,' said Amrit.

'What if you don't find the owner's name?' Amrit continued.

'We will follow in your footsteps and hand the earrings over to the National Museum. Will you help us in donating it, as we are not aware of the process?' said Ajji.

'Yes, of course. You can keep my phone number. I can guide you,' Amrit assured her.

Both Ajja and Ajji heaved a sigh—the earrings were a great responsibility, and they wanted to ensure they ended up in the right hands.

Nooni gave Amrit a detailed description. He began searching for: A pair of earrings, peacock design, studded with red rubies . . .

To everyone's surprise, the description matched, and a photo appeared on the screen. It was an exact replica of the pair that Nooni had, only in red rubies. There was even a note in the remarks column:

The Magic of the Lost Earrings

Estimated to be from the 1850s, during the reign of Maharaja Ranjit Singh. Seller's name: Daman Kaur, 885 Circular Road, Amritsar.

It was the first time they had something solid. They now knew a lady by the name of Daman Kaur had sold the first pair of earrings, and they had her address. They thanked Amrit, who invited them to stay for tea. But their hearts were full of hope, and they were ready to take the next step. With quiet determination, they took their leave and continued their journey.

The Next Piece of the Puzzle

On the way to Daman Kaur's house, Nooni wondered if, somewhere, there was an old lady who owned two pairs of earrings. Nooni felt the earrings must be so precious, and something must have forced her to sell one pair a long time ago. She also wondered how heartbroken Daman Kaur must be to lose even the second pair.

Searching for Daman Kaur's house was not difficult; getting there was the hard part. Narrow lanes and gullies were filled with crowds and vehicles on both sides. Though a small footpath ran along the road, it was mostly taken over by roadside vendors.

With great difficulty, Nooni and her grandparents reached the correct address. There was a mattress shop next to a small house. They rang the bell, and a young man opened it. He saw them and said, 'The shop is next door, please come.'

Ajja stopped and said, 'No, we have not come to buy a mattress. We want to meet Daman Kaur ji.'

'What?' He was surprised.

'Yes, we want to meet Daman Kaur ji,' insisted Ajji.

'We have come all the way from the south,' stressed Nooni.

'*Beta*, why are you making customers stand outside the house while talking to them?' said a voice from the back. 'Call them in.'

'Nani ji, they are not customers, but they have come to meet you.'

'Then they are our guests. Please call them in,' said the voice from inside.

The young man opened both sides of the door, and all three stepped in hesitantly.

Nooni looked around with curiosity. There was a small courtyard with a charpoy in the middle. An old sofa and a few chairs were arranged nearby, and three or four doors opened into the courtyard. The interior of the house was modest with flashy colours. There was kirtan playing softly on the TV.

An old lady with a colourful dupatta sat peeling green peas on the charpoy. She was surprised to

see them and welcomed them in Punjabi, 'Please, sit down.'

Then she switched to Hindi. 'What can I offer you, hot milk or chai?'

Her warmth made them smile.

Ajja only requested for water, but the old lady sent the young man to bring tea and biscuits for everyone.

Then turning to her guests, she asked, 'May I know who you are? And why have you come to meet me?'

Ajji thought to herself that if she had lost the earrings, she wouldn't have been so calm.

But Ajja introduced himself and asked politely, 'Have you lost anything precious at the Bangalore airport about a week ago?'

Daman looked confused. 'I've never travelled to the south. I don't even know where Bangalore is. I've spent my entire life in the north. Occasionally, I've been to Chandigarh, Delhi, Ludhiana and Jalandhar for weddings or pilgrimages. I know there's a place called Nanak Jhira in the south, somewhere near Bidar, but I've never managed to go that far. What brought you here, to meet an unknown person like me?'

Her words left all three of them surprised—and a little disheartened. They didn't know how to carry the conversation forward. Ajji was cautious not to reveal too much, but Nooni, being an innocent child, blurted out, 'Did you lose any special earrings somewhere?'

'No, I don't have any special earrings, and I've never lost any,' she replied, gently shaking her head.

Nooni then remembered the red stone earrings and asked, 'Did you ever sell any special earrings a long time ago?'

'I don't recall doing so,' said Daman.

She turned to Ajji and continued, 'We're from Amritsar and have been living in this house for generations. We've never moved away. We've always lived a simple life and never owned anything expensive. My father started this mattress business, and I inherited it from him. I passed it on to my daughter, and now her son manages it. We're content with our lives and our work. But your questions are puzzling. If you're not here to buy a mattress, how did you find us—and why did you come looking for me in particular?'

'We got your address from Amrit Ram,' said Ajja.

Daman Kaur looked even more puzzled. 'Who is Amrit Ram? I've never heard that name before,' she replied.

Just then, the same young man appeared, carrying a tray with glasses of water, tea and biscuits, which he placed before them with a polite smile.

Once again, Daman asked, 'What are these earrings you're talking about that have brought you all the way here?'

'We visited Kewal Bazaar. Amrit Ram, the grandson of Professor Kewal Ram, gave us your name. Professor Kewal Ram once lived at the *chauraha* where the Kewal Bazaar now stands. He used to collect antique gold ornaments. Apparently, he paid double their worth. We found your name and address in his records. Do you recall anything about him?'

Daman Kaur appeared deep in thought. After a few minutes, she said, 'Oh, that professor sahib! Of course, I remember him. I visited his house many years ago. It's all coming back slowly. Perhaps when Bharati finished her matriculation. Yes, we were classmates—she got first class, and I just passed.'

Daman Kaur relaxed, and it seemed like she was talking to herself.

She turned to Ajji. 'We had a small house next door to this one. We've turned it into a store now. Many years ago, we had a tenant, a schoolteacher by the name of Simran Kaur. She had a sister by the name of Bharati Kaur.'

Daman paused to sip her tea and then continued, 'Bharati was an unusual name for a girl in Punjab. She was born on the day of India's Independence, which is why she was named Bharati. She was a bright girl, and Simran was ten years older than her. Their parents were very old and quiet. Bharati and I were the same age and studied together till matriculation. Simran used to tell me that they had come from a village near the India–Pakistan border, walking across to settle here. They lived in different refugee camps before finding a home.

'Their father was a reserved man who worked as a manager at Harmandir Sahib. Their mother rarely spoke but was skilled at embroidery; that was how she earned a living. Once, Simran told me that they had been quite well off in their village but had to leave everything behind during Partition, which brought them many hardships.

'Bharati became a nurse and later went abroad. It was hard for her to leave her baby and husband behind. He worked in the pharmaceutical industry. Simran did a great deal for her family—she raised the child, worked as a teacher, managed the household and cared for her ageing parents. She truly shouldered everything.'

'What happened to Simran Kaur?' asked Nooni.

'Simran gave up her personal dreams for her family. She never married so she could take care of them. I heard that Bharati, too, faced many difficulties abroad, but eventually got a good job.'

'Do you have any contact with them now?' asked Ajja.

'No, we lost touch. But just a few days ago, Simran surprised me and came to visit. She is aged now. She said that she had come to offer her prayers at Harmandir Sahib. Rab has been very kind to her. Bharati's son has done well. She stayed only for half an hour. Both of us remembered our school days and her parents. They struggled a lot but never saw better times. And then she left.'

'Do you have her address?' Nooni asked again.

'No. I didn't ask, and she didn't share it with me,' Daman replied.

'By any chance, do you remember which country she lives in?'

'No . . . maybe she said the UK or USA. I don't remember clearly.'

'Why did you go to Kewal Ram all those years ago?' asked Nooni again.

Though quite old, Daman Kaur looked very healthy and sharp. She adjusted her pillow and said, 'Yes, I forgot to tell you. When Bharati wanted to join nursing after her matriculation, her family didn't have the money to pay the course fee. Simran one day came to me and said, "Bharati wants to become a doctor. She's bright, but we can't afford her education. So, she has chosen nursing instead—it's still in the medical field. But even paying for that is difficult for us. I have decided to sell my precious earrings. They're a family heirloom. I always kept them with great care, and now the time has come because we really don't have money. I have kept them safe all my life, but now Bharati's education is at stake. She is bright, and I have decided to sell my precious earrings for the sake of my sister's education."

'Simran didn't want to go to a jeweller herself. As they were from a well-off family, they were emotionally attached to their belongings. Though Simran was ten years older than me, I had a better sense of bargaining as we were in business. So, my father and I got the earrings evaluated. In those times, there weren't a lot of jewellers in Amritsar. One helpful jeweller advised us to try Professor Kewal Ram, who loved antiques. He gave us Kewal Ram's address, and we went to his bungalow. He was very kind. He asked repeatedly if I was sure. When we explained the situation, he paid double the value and even more, as he believed in education.'

Simran's story brought tears to Ajji's eyes. Sometimes the personal sacrifices we make for our loved ones are so much bigger than any hardship.

'Did you give your address there?' Nooni asked.

'Yes. As Simran was our tenant at that time. So, we gave our address as Kewal Ram was keen on documenting the information while acquiring any antique item. He had a register in which he wrote down my address. Those were simpler times, so he didn't need any other proof or documents. That's all. But still, I am not able to understand why you want all this information. Do you know Bharati? Who has sent you to me?'

Everyone could see Daman's puzzled expression.

'By mistake a pair of earrings came into our possession. While tracing the rightful owner, we found that there was another pair in a different colour—which you just told us about. We believe Simran Kaur might be that person who perhaps owned both the pairs, one of which was sold to Kewal Ram,' Ajji replied.

'Maybe,' Daman said slowly.

As you piece together the jigsaw, the magic of the lost earrings begins to take shape on its own.

'So close, yet so far,' Nooni sighed.

Now they knew about Simran Kaur and her sister Bharati Kaur, who was a nurse. They had emigrated abroad. They now knew Simran Kaur had another pair of earrings—this one with green emeralds. They had traced them back to her but didn't know where she lived now. It could be the US or the UK, as Daman was not sure where Bharati had moved; it would be difficult for them to find out.

When they were about to leave, Ajji asked as a last resort, 'Do you know anyone who might have any information about Bharati Kaur?'

Daman, lost in thought, replied, 'Perhaps you can try meeting Mary D'Souza. She was our classmate, a dear friend of Bharati. Her father ran the Mission School, and we all studied there together. Bharati stood first in class, Mary got second class, and I had just passed. Mary and Bharati wanted to pursue medicine, but they became nurses. They were good friends and had worked together, whereas I got married and got busy with my own family. When my children grew up, they went to a nearby school, so I never got a chance to stay in touch with the D'Souzas.'

'Is that mission school still there?' Nooni quickly asked.

'Yes, it is an old but well-known school. After Father D'Souza passed away, Mary took over, and she now works there as the financial administrator.'

'How do you know this?' Nooni's questions were increasing.

'Recently, the school had sent out invitations for the centenary celebration to all former students, and even I had received one. I went there and met Mary after so many years. She told me that she has been working at the school. We remembered Bharati, too.'

'Can we meet Mary D'Souza?' asked Nooni, with a tensed voice.

'You can try. The Mission School is on the way to the airport. You can just walk in and ask for the financial administrator. Like her father, she lives in the same compound,' Daman replied.

The three of them didn't realize how much time had passed while listening to Daman Kaur.

They thanked her for sharing so much with them. Though she invited them to have lunch with her, they politely declined. Eager to meet Mary D'Souza, they left.

'May Wahe Guru bless them. In this greedy world, there are still some pious people who want to return what is not theirs. That is why rains still fall and crops still grow,' Daman said to her grandson.

Delhi Adventures

On the way to the airport, Ajji insisted they try to meet Mary D'Souza, but Ajja was not keen. 'Again we will go there and find out another story. How long can we go on searching like this? Let's stop here.'

But Ajji ignored him and said, 'Try and try again boys; you will succeed at last. Remember Lord Tennyson's poem? It is meant for all of us. And anyway, it's on the way to the airport.'

They followed the address and reached a huge compound with a new board that read: 'Mission School Centenary Celebration', indicating that the school was still basking in the glory of the recent event.

It was an old colonial-style stone building with high ceilings and red floor tiles. There was a huge playground with a small chapel at one corner.

The school was surrounded by many neem trees with thick trunks. The flowering branches swayed gently in the breeze.

As it was a Saturday, the school was quiet, but the office was open.

Hesitantly, all three of them entered the building. An office boy carrying a tiffin box walked past. Ajja stopped him. 'Can you please direct us to the financial administrator, Ms Mary D'Souza's office?'

'Do you mean the bursar? Yes, you can follow the main corridor; it will be on your left.' He pointed to the round, yellow-coloured building.

Ajja and Ajji looked puzzled. Immediately, Nooni quickly checked on her phone and said, 'Ajji, "bursar" is a British term. It means a person who manages the financial affairs of an institution. Probably here, it refers to the office of the finance administrator.'

They walked over to the round building. A nameplate read: 'Ms Mary D'Souza'.

A young receptionist greeted them and asked, 'Do you have an appointment?'

'We have come from Bangalore. We'd like to meet Ms D'Souza. However, we don't have an appointment,' said Ajja.

The receptionist checked with Ms D'Souza and then waved them in.

Inside, a lady who looked like she was in her sixties looked up from her book.

Ajja introduced himself, Ajji and Nooni and said, 'We won't take much of your time. We are on our way to the airport. Do you remember Bharati Kaur, your old classmate and colleague who was a nurse?'

Mary D'Souza was taken aback. 'Yes! I remember her. That was a long time ago, though. How may I help you?'

She offered them tea.

'We just want to know where she is living now,' replied Ajja.

'Oh, I am sorry. I really don't know that. I haven't seen her for years. We studied together. We both went to the same college, and after our degrees, we worked together for a couple of years. Then we saw an advertisement for nurses needed in the UK. It was a hospital in Aberdeen, in a small village where it's extremely cold. Bharati applied and got selected. I didn't apply, as I wasn't willing to go to a cold country, all alone, to work in a remote area. I was comfortable in Amritsar. But Bharati was brave. She went ahead. I heard later

that she took her family with her, too. Bharati worked hard. She must be well settled now. But we lost touch. Recently, we wanted to invite all our former students to the centenary celebration, but since we didn't have any contact for Bharati, we couldn't invite her.'

'Is she still in the UK?' Ajji asked.

'I don't know that. Initially, she wrote letters, but over a period of time, even that stopped. I became a matron here and eventually retired. I wanted to help our school even after I retired. Life gets busy, and it becomes difficult to keep in touch,' Mary replied.

Then she asked, 'By the way, may I please ask why you are looking for Bharati? Do you know her?'

'In a way, I know her,' smiled Nooni.

Mary D'Souza didn't ask anything further.

The three of them were in a hurry as they had to catch a flight, so they thanked her for helping them with all the information she had. Then they hurried to the airport.

Nooni's mind was buzzing. They now knew Simran Kaur had a younger sister, Bharati Kaur, who was a staff nurse and had a son. The family had moved to the UK. If they were still there, it might be possible to find them as they had an upcoming trip. But if the sisters had moved elsewhere, it might be impossible.

They were preparing to go to Delhi from Amritsar. Every time they got close to finding the owner, they hit another dead end. But in just one week, they had seen so much of India—its culture, people and stories. Along with the great responsibility of handing over the lost earrings to the real owner, they had also witnessed the pain of the refugees, their helplessness and their courage.

Ajja now felt that meeting Daman Kaur might be the end of the search. Since the earrings clearly did not belong to her, perhaps the best thing would be to donate them to a museum, as Amrit Ram had done, with a label: 'Owned by Simran Kaur'.

Ajji quietly agreed. She felt that in India, people often know each other's personal histories, as they socialize a lot. Additionally, they were more familiar with India. Searching for Simran in London after so long would be incredibly difficult. Maybe Simran and Bharati were still in the UK—or maybe not.

By and large, Ajji also felt it was a waste of time to investigate further. She was of the same opinion as Ajja—that they could hand over the earrings to the department of antiquities at the National Museum, New Delhi. Amrit Ram had offered to help them with the procedure, too.

Although Ajji and Ajja were ready to stop, Nooni had different thoughts.

As she was very young and more enthusiastic, hopeful and perhaps a little impractical, Nooni believed it was possible to trace Simran Kaur in the UK.

In case they did not have any luck in London, they could always give the earrings to the museum. In the last few days, they had checked with the airport authorities in Bangalore, and there no incident of missing jewellery had been reported. So, they thought it would be ideal to donate the earrings, in case they could not locate Simran Kaur in the UK.

'Nooni, we will support you. You focus on your exams for the next two months. I will keep these earrings with me. We will continue our search when we go to London. But don't share all these details with anyone. These are antique pieces, and we must be careful. You can tell your parents, but no one else.'

They arrived in Delhi the following morning.

It was Nooni's choice to visit the capital. Ajja and Ajji had seen Delhi before, but the city had changed so much over the years.

Since it was Nooni's first time, Ajji took the opportunity to share her love for the city's history.

'Nooni,' she began, 'if you truly want to see Delhi, you should see it in parts. It has been the capital of many empires across centuries. Mythologically, it was Indraprastha, built on the banks of the river Yamuna. Later, it became the capital of Prithviraj, and that area was called Qila Rai Pithora. After that, it passed to the Sultans, then to the Tughlaqs, who built Tughlaqabad. Later, it became Shahjahanabad under the Mughals, which we now call Old Delhi. Under British rule, it became Lutyens's Delhi. And after Independence, it came to be known as New Delhi.'

Impressed, Ajja raised an eyebrow. 'Is there any proof of all this?'

'Yes,' Ajji said with confidence. 'Every ruler left behind monuments in Delhi—from Purana Qila to Sansad Bhawan. Even our new Parliament building adds to this rich, vibrant history.'

'So what can we see in the next two or three days, Ajji?' Nooni asked eagerly.

'Let's see the Qutb Minar, the Red Fort, Chandni Chowk and the Prime Minister's Museum this time. But remember, whatever you see, let it stay with you. For that matter, just like Madhya Pradesh, you have to visit Delhi at least four or five times to cover its vast heritage.'

Under Ajji's guidance, their first stop was the Qutb Minar. The tall, beautiful structure stood proudly against the blue sky. A few tourist guides approached them, offering to explain the monument's history.

Ajja waved them off. 'We have our own history teacher who can probably take a class here,' he joked.

Ajji smiled and said, 'There are many folk tales about the Qutb Minar. Some say it was built by Maharaja Prithviraj Chauhan for his wife Sanyukta, who was a great devotee of the river Yamuna. She would climb to the top of the minar for a daily *darshan* of the river. But historically, it was built by Qutb-ud-din Aibak, the Sultan of Delhi and grandfather of Razia Sultana, the only female ruler of Delhi.'

Nearby, they saw an iron pillar. Ajji stopped and explained, 'This is remarkable. It seems this iron pillar is approximately seven metres tall,

with a diameter of about forty centimetres. It was constructed by Chandragupta II of the Gupta dynasty. The metal used here is rust resistant. It shows how advanced ancient Indians were in metallurgy.'

Nooni took pictures and even made Ajja-Ajji pose for them.

From there, they went to the Red Fort.

'This entire area,' said Ajji, 'was built by the Mughal Emperor Shah Jahan, and it was called Shahjahanabad. The red sandstone gives the fort its name. It's massive inside. The Mughals ruled from here until the British took over in 1857.'

'Ajji, there are so many buildings inside,' said Nooni, looking around in awe.

'Yes, the emperor and his court lived here. The royal women stayed in an enclosed section called *zanana*.'

Ajji led them into a large hall and said, 'This is the Diwan-i-Aam, where the emperor held court for the public.' She pointed to the raised platform. 'That's where the emperor sat.'

Nooni quickly took some more photos.

'I remember hearing about a peacock throne made up of many diamonds and precious stones,' said Ajja.

'Yes, it was kept right here until it was taken to Iran by Nadir Shah during one of the invasions.'

They wandered further and reached a marble building.

'This is the Diwan-i-Khas. Here, the emperor met his private guests. Notice the marble channels running through the hall,' said Ajji.

'What are all these channels for?' asked Nooni.

'Delhi gets scorching in summer, so the Mughals arranged for cool water from the Yamuna River to flow through these channels and cool the palace interiors.'

There was something written on the marble wall that caught their eye.

Ajji laughed and said, 'This is part of the grandeur of Mughal architecture. As the famous line goes: *Agar firdaus bar roo-e zameen ast, hameen ast-o hameen ast-o hameen ast*, meaning, "If there is a paradise on earth, it is this, it is this, it is this."'

Nooni smiled at that.

The journey continued to Chandni Chowk.

'I know Chandni Chowk better than Ajji,' Ajja said proudly. 'I was posted here for a short duration. There's a street called Paranthe Wali Gali that's over a hundred years old. *Dharti pe khana hai to yahi hai, yahi hai*—meaning, "If there's good food on earth, it is here, it is here"' Ajja joked.

'Chandni Chowk was designed by Princess Jahanara, daughter of Shah Jahan,' he added.

'Every faith has a home here—an ancient Jain mandir, a Mahadev mandir, the Shish Ganj Gurudwara, Fatehpuri Masjid and even a Central Baptist Church,' Ajji added. 'You can buy anything and everything in Chandni Chowk,' she declared.

'Yes, except Ajji's love,' smiled Ajja.

They all laughed.

They walked over to a shop and squeezed on to a busy bench, sharing hot chole bhature and sweet, sticky jalebis.

Nooni grinned and said, 'This is yummy!'

After eating wholeheartedly at Chandni Chowk, they set off for the Prime Minister's Museum. The museum is located at Teen Murti Bhavan. Ajji

pointed out the three statues at the traffic circle. 'These are soldiers,' she explained. 'This place gets its name, Teen Murti, from them.'

Inside, they saw an old colonial-style building that was once the residence of Jawaharlal Nehru, India's first prime minister. At the back, it was connected to a large, modern building filled with exhibits on all of India's prime ministers and their achievements.

Nooni enjoyed this part the most—it had lots of fun, interactive displays and used exciting new technologies!

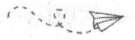

On the last day, just before their flight back to Bangalore, Nooni had one final wish.

She wanted to visit the National Museum to check about the other pair of earrings that Amrit Ram had talked about.

Ajji was not convinced.

'What will that achieve, Nooni? It will not give us the real owner's address. Anything you see in the photo is no different from seeing with your eyes,' said Ajji.

'But let's go for Nooni's sake,' said Ajja gently.

All of them then visited the National Museum in Delhi. It was vast, with artefacts from the Indus Valley to modern-day India. Gold, bronze, terracotta, coins from Kushana, Gupta and Mughal periods also adorned the halls of the museum.

Ajji was in her element. She spoke to Nooni about each and every object with great enthusiasm.

'Nooni, this is the best place to learn about a country's history,' Ajji told Nooni.

Ajji then pointed to one of the exhibits—it was an old coin from the time of Sher Shah Suri, with rupayya written beneath it. 'Look! Sher Shah Suri, who built the Grand Trunk Road from Calcutta to Peshawar, also introduced the word *rupayya*. The original rupee weighed 11.66 grams.'

'Ajji,' Nooni interrupted softly, 'shall we go and see the ornaments of Maharaja Ranjit Singh?'

Ajja-Ajji nodded. They went through the entire museum and found the Sikh history section. They saw different *bazubands*, *sarpechs*, garlands of pearls and rubies, bangles—but no earrings.

Nooni's face fell.

Ajja cajoled her and said, 'Let's ask the curator of the museum. Nooni, did you take a photo of the earrings from Amrit Ram's file?'

'Yes, but it is not very clear. I wish I could see the red earrings with my own eyes,' said Nooni.

They went to the curator's office. He was examining an antique object through a magnifying glass.

They introduced themselves and said, 'We are from Bangalore. Our granddaughter has a specific question. Will you help us out?'

The curator's face lit up. He said, 'How wonderful to see a young visitor so curious! Museums are full of stories. These artefacts are silent witnesses to our past. They tell stories of peace and war and of the lifestyle of any society. If only objects could talk, what they could reveal!'

Nooni stepped forward and showed him the photo of the earrings on her phone. She said, 'I took this photo from Mr Amrit Ram of Amritsar. It seems these earrings were donated to your museum. They are from Maharaja Ranjit Singh's reign. There is also an inscription at the back to authenticate that. I wanted to see the earrings, but I could not find them in the collection of Maharaja Ranjit Singh.'

The curator chuckled and said, 'What you see in a museum is just the tip of the iceberg. Most of our collection is safely stored and shown in turns. Some pieces are sent on tours, and we call them "travelling exhibits". Similarly, we also receive objects from museums abroad. Did you see this month's special exhibit?'

'No, what is it?' asked Nooni.

'This month, the Cairo Museum has sent a mummy and some alabaster jars from the Ramesside period. It is the attraction of this month. Please go and have a look.'

'Yes, we will. But can you please tell us if we can see these earrings?' Nooni showed him the photo again.

The curator turned to his computer. Typing quickly, he said, 'Earlier, we maintained paper files. They were hard to manage and often got damaged. Now, everything is digitized. Thanks to the no-paper policy, records are well kept.'

'Look,' he said, turning the monitor towards Nooni, 'here they are! All the details are catalogued here, including the number of stones, sizes, inscription and origin, among others. These earrings were generously donated by Mr Amrit Ram. We appreciate people like him who give items from their collection to the country's archival museums—such items are our national treasures.'

'Can I see them?' asked Nooni.

'Not right now. They're not here.'

Nooni frowned.

'Don't be upset,' he immediately said. 'They've been sent to New York as part of a travelling exhibition titled "Earrings from a Different Era". They will be back in India after a year or so. The exhibition from New York will go to Paris, then

Vienna, then London, Dubai and finally return to India.'

'Isn't it risky to send delicate, valuable items like these abroad?' asked Ajja.

'Yes, absolutely. We take great care and work hard to ensure they are sent with complete safety and protection for such exhibitions. It is not easy. However, it's worth it. We still participate so that people who cannot visit India can see a glimpse of India's great heritage through these exhibitions. Similarly, we also get exhibits from around the world so that our people can see a part of world history.'

'That's wonderful! When will the earrings reach London?' asked Nooni, already calculating dates in her head.

'In about two months. They'll be displayed at the Victoria and Albert Museum for two weeks.'

To her surprise, this time it was coinciding with her England travel dates.

'We might be in London around that time,' said Ajja. 'God willing, we'll see them there.'

They thanked the curator and stepped out. Nooni felt a little more hopeful.

London Calling

The following morning, they flew to Bangalore.

The pair of earrings remained safely tucked inside Ajji's purse. While travelling, Ajji turned to Nooni and said, 'Nooni, let's not lose hope. We will find a way to search for Bharati and Simran Kaur in the UK and hand over their earrings. Don't worry.'

'Ajji thinks London is like Somanahalli! But she is right; let's not lose hope,' Ajja joked.

For the next two months, Nooni was busy with her studies. Her father was occupied arranging visas for Nooni, Ajja and Ajji. Radha, her aunt in London, sent the sponsorship letters.

Nooni's mother, Usha, sat Nooni down and said, 'It costs a lot of money to travel to London. Though your group has been selected, and the department of culture is covering it, you will still require money for sightseeing in London and for other expenses. We shouldn't ask Radha for any financial help—that wouldn't be right. Ajja and Ajji are using their savings they had kept aside for their pilgrimage to buy these tickets. So, Nooni, this year there will be no gifts for you. Instead, I will send that money to Ajja and Ajji to help with the London trip. Nothing is free in life, Nooni, and you must value hard-earned money.'

Nooni nodded immediately. She didn't want any gifts; she was thrilled about the London trip with Ajja and Ajji.

'But Amma, there is something that is free in life,' she said.

Usha raised her eyebrows and asked, 'What is that? I have never heard or seen anything like that.'

Nooni hugged her mother and said, 'You have experienced it and enjoyed it. It is a mother's love, which is free, unconditional and endless.'

Usha smiled softly and hugged Nooni.

The weeks flew by quickly. Nooni's exams ended, her troupe rehearsals were in full swing, and final

preparations for the London trip had begun. Before she knew it, the day of their travel had arrived.

Ajja and Ajji came to Bangalore from Somanahalli. Ajji had brought along a rather heavy suitcase.

Seeing this, Shekhar, Nooni's father, said, 'Amma, don't carry so much luggage. In economy, only twenty-three kilograms are allowed. And in London, all Indian items are easily available. Don't make your luggage too heavy.'

Ajji was disappointed. 'Oh, I was carrying homemade pappad, vermicelli, pickle, sambar powder and such things for Radha. I have some fresh vegetables like drumsticks, round brinjals and so on. We have some excellent-quality rice this year. I thought I would take at least five kilograms for her. How will I manage now?'

Ajja added dryly, 'Apart from that, she has packed saris, dhotis, heavy winter clothes and a bunch of books to read—though I repeatedly told her not to!'

Usha stepped in with a gentle explanation. 'I understand Amma's concern. But since this is your first time flying abroad, you may not know

that carrying vegetables, plants and seeds is not allowed. And since it's May, the weather won't be that cold. Amma, you can manage with light winter wear. The pickle bottle might break, even if packed well. Don't carry too many books; just take a couple for the flight. I will help you repack everything within the weight limit.'

Ajji sighed but didn't protest. She was quietly disappointed, but she knew Usha was right.

Ajja had travelled abroad once in his short military stint. But for Ajji and Nooni, it was their maiden trip.

Nooni, meanwhile, had packed sensibly. Her dance troupe had given strict instructions on what was permitted and what wasn't, so she had no trouble. Ajja, as always, travelled light. Shekhar made sure all three of them had international roaming on their mobile phones and patiently explained how to use it economically.

Soon, it was time to leave for the airport. Usha and Shekhar went to the airport to drop everyone off.

Usha slipped a small pouch in to her Amma's bag and said, 'I have kept some basic medicines here. Seeing a doctor abroad isn't easy, and I just want you to be prepared.'

Usha hugged Nooni tightly and said, 'Take as many photos as you like and share them with us. You will be in London for two weeks. The first four days will go in your rehearsals and jet lag, and you will be staying with your dance group. After that, you will shift to Radha's house. Practise well with full concentration. If you work hard, results will follow. Your main goal is to perform classical Indian dance and showcase it to the Western world. And have a good trip, my child. Happy journey!'

'No,' said Nooni with a smile. 'Apart from dance, I have one more important thing.'

Everyone turned to look at her, surprised by her answer.

'I also have to search for the owner of the earrings!' said Nooni, excitedly.

During the flight, Ajji appeared a little disappointed. She looked around at the narrow seats and said, 'I thought international flights would be more spacious. These economy seats are very much like our domestic ones in India.'

But Ajji was very happy to see the food menu. 'Oh, I can eat bisi bele anna, Karnataka's speciality, on a flight to London!' she beamed.

The three of them sat together in one row. Ajji had the window seat, Ajja took the aisle, and Nooni sat in between them so she could talk to both.

Their journey had begun not just to another country, but perhaps to the heart of an old mystery still waiting to be solved.

As the flight cruised high above the clouds, Ajja gazed out thoughtfully. The soft hum of the aeroplane reminded him of his own journey abroad many decades ago.

'Things have changed so much in fifty years. When I travelled back then, people had very little information about India,' Ajja said.

Nooni thought for a moment, then asked, 'What do you think now, Ajja?'

Ajja smiled at Nooni's question and replied, 'I feel India has changed a lot. Our youngsters are more confident than we ever were. Many countries now know about India—not just as a land of heritage but also as a place of innovation and hard work. It is because of Indians who've carried our values across the world: a no-nonsense attitude, paying taxes honestly, working with dedication.

These qualities have changed how the world sees India.'

He looked around the cabin and continued, 'In those days, if we wanted to watch a movie on a plane, we had to pay three dollars just to rent the headphones. Today, even in economy class, we can enjoy Indian food, watch movies for free, and more than that, the entire flight is full of Indians. That makes me very proud.'

The long flight eventually came to an end. It was a direct flight. As it touched down at Heathrow Airport, the three of them peered out of the windows, taking in the new country with quiet excitement. The airport was vast and bustling, filled with voices and people from every part of the world.

'You can hear all kinds of languages spoken in the world at this airport,' said Ajja, glancing around. 'This is one of the world's busiest and most well-connected airports. It's like a crossroads of the globe.'

When they came out with their luggage, Radha was waiting for them. When she saw Ajja and Ajji at the exit, she touched their feet and hugged them.

'Oh, Mami! I'm seeing you after so many years. I'm so happy you finally made it to London. Welcome!' she said, her voice warm with affection.

Then Radha turned to Nooni. 'Is it really Anoushka? I last saw you when you were five years old; it has been such a long time. These days, there are good connecting flights to Hubli, my hometown, from Bangalore, so I don't need to stay in the city at all.'

Ajja was very happy to see his niece after so many years. Radha loaded their luggage into the car, and soon, the four of them were on the way to Radha's house.

As she drove, Radha glanced at Ajja in the rear-view mirror and said, 'I have heard about Nooni's adventures. I read about how she discovered the stepwell at the Somanahalli Temple. Mami had sent me newspaper cuttings. And I watched her interview on the Internet!'

'Yes, Radha, Nooni is a bright girl. Not only that, she also traced our family history. I had written to you about the Yashoda–Krishna Temple, remember?

'Oh, she is truly an adventurous girl,' Radha said warmly.

Nooni felt shy at all the praise.

'So, what is your next adventure then?' Radha asked, glancing at Nooni through the mirror.

'Apart from my dance performance at Bharatiya Vidya Bhavan, I have also come here to solve another puzzle. Ajja-Ajji will explain that to you at home,' replied Nooni.

Soon, they all were home and had a hearty lunch.

Later that day, Ajja told Radha the complete plan. 'Nooni has come here to perform at Bharatiya Vidya Bhavan, often called BVB. All her teammates are arriving in London today. Tonight, they will assemble at BVB, where accommodation has been arranged for three days. After their performance, they can either return to India or stay back with family or friends. It's their choice.'

Radha was looking forward to the next few weeks with Ajja, Ajji and Nooni.

That evening, Radha drove the three of them to BVB to drop Nooni off.

Bharatiya Vidya Bhavan or BVB, is the cultural heart of the Indian community in London. It is headed by Mattur Nandakumar, a well-respected connoisseur of Indian arts, music, dance and literature.

The building had a spacious auditorium and was buzzing with energy. The organization conducted regular classes in veena, violin, tabla, vocal music, sitar and more. On weekends, students came in for classical dance classes in Bharatnatyam, Kuchipudi and Kathak. Many young students, including foreigners, came to learn and appreciate Indian arts.

BVB also hosted eight-week-long summer courses, where experts from India were invited to teach. Throughout the year, cultural troupes from India were invited to perform, giving students and local audiences a chance to experience live performances by professional Indian artistes.

Nooni's troupe, comprising seven students and their teacher, had been invited to perform a Kuchipudi recital. They had prepared a series of pieces based on different themes—Krishna and Satyabhama, Krishna and Yashoda, Goddess Durga, and the celebration of the spring festival. Each dance required a different costume, so the team was travelling with a lot of luggage.

Ajja-Ajji could see all the young girls running around with great enthusiasm. They hugged their granddaughter and left. Nooni was excited for the next few days at BVB.

Exploring and Discovering

Back at home, after a warm meal and some rest, Ajji began narrating the story of the lost earrings to Radha in full detail. Ajja decided to take a nap because he already knew this story.

Radha listened intently. She was surprised at the perseverance and integrity of the couple and young Nooni—travelling such a great distance just to try to return something that wasn't theirs.

'Mami, I'll help you,' Radha said firmly. 'Even though Bharati is a nurse, there's no guarantee she's still in London. She may have retired by now or moved anywhere in the UK—maybe Wales or Scotland. It's a small island compared to India, but still quite spread out.'

She paused and added, 'I know Nandakumar and his wife, Janaki, quite well. They are wonderful people. I am also a member of BVB. I attend lectures there and regularly go to the Diwali banquet. Many Indians do come to BVB, and we can take their help to trace Simran and Bharati. After Nooni's performance, we will meet Nandakumar, and I'm sure some solution will come out of it.'

Over the next few days, Radha had planned to take Ajja and Ajji out to explore a new place each day.

Ajji was especially curious about how Indians lived in London.

One morning, she asked, 'Radha, how do our people manage in a foreign country like this?'

Radha smiled, 'I will take you to Ealing Market tomorrow. You will feel like you are walking through a market in Bangalore.'

The next day, they took the London tube to go to Ealing Market.

When they reached Ealing and stepped into one of the Indian shops, Ajji was astonished. Every variety of papad, pickle, spice powder and Indian condiment was neatly arranged on the shelves and available at a reasonable price. There was a section

for dosa and idli batter, even half-cooked parathas of different types. The vegetable section was filled with all the familiar items from home—and some that Ajji had never even seen in Somanahalli. There was even fresh jasmine, which she promptly bought and pinned in her hair with a smile.

Impressed, Ajji told Ajja, 'Now I understand why you told me not to carry anything from home!'

The following day, Ajji's curiosity shifted again.

'Do they have temples here? And gurdwaras? What about mosques? Places where people can pray?' she asked.

Radha laughed and said, 'Mami, you will find everything here. London is truly a cosmopolitan city and a global financial hub. People from every corner of the world live here, and the government provides facilities for everyone to practice their religion freely. You'll see temples, gurdwaras, mosques and even spiritual centres like the Ramakrishna Mission and Chinmaya Mission. We will visit a few places of worship during your stay here.'

'Today, I'll take you to the Shree Ghanapathy Temple in Wimbledon,' Radha added.

Ajja's face lit up with excitement. 'Yes, we should go. I'm very excited to see the Wimbledon courts, too. There are two places in London which we absolutely must not miss—Lord's cricket ground and the Wimbledon courts. Lord's is where cricketing legends are made. Though there are many grand tennis tournaments like the French Open and the Australian Open, Wimbledon is the crown jewel—it's produced some of the greatest tennis champions in the world.'

That day, they went to the temple. It was spacious and welcoming.

As soon as they entered, Ajji said, 'Apart from Lord Ganesha, there are so many other gods here.'

Radha smiled and said, 'Yes, Mami, it's not possible to build separate temples for each deity here. So, many temples in the UK have multiple shrines. Devotees who worship different gods—be it Lord Ram, Krishna, Ishwar or Devi—can all come to one place. They offer prayers to Vinayaka and also to their chosen deity. We celebrate many festivals like Ram Navami, Janmashtami, Shivaratri, Ganesh Chaturthi, Durgashtami, even Srinivasa Kalyanam, and many more here. On festival days, we prepare and serve lunch to all the devotees.'

Ajji was particularly delighted when she found out that the temple's priest was from Karnataka.

'Yes, Mami. The *archakas*, the cooks and many of the temple workers come here on special visas. Their roles are considered skilled and essential,' Radha explained.

Ajji was impressed.

The temple was abuzz with activity. In one section, a child was performing *aksharabhyasa* — tracing letters in a tray of raw rice as part of their first learning ritual. Nearby, a baby's *mundan* ceremony was taking place, where a child's first haircut is offered to the deity. In the adjacent hall, there was a sacred *upanayanam* (thread ceremony) being conducted, and in another corner, a small wedding was underway.

Ajji stood quietly for a moment, taking it all in.

'It's such a beautiful system,' she finally said. 'Even though you are far from home, you're still keeping our traditions alive. It feels like a little piece of India, right here in London.'

Then they headed to fulfil Ajja's wish, to see the Wimbledon tennis stadium.

At the entrance, they discovered the ticket price was quite steep.

Ajji raised an eyebrow and asked, 'Why should we pay to see an empty ground?'

Radha smiled and explained, 'It's not just an empty ground, Mami. Thousands of people visit every year. They have to maintain the lawns and gardens and provide security and guides—it all adds up. The ticket helps to cover those costs.'

They purchased their tickets, which included a guided tour. The guide began by explaining the history of the grounds.

'Wimbledon began as a small local tournament in this suburb of London, played initially only by the English elite. Over time, it evolved into one of the most prestigious international tennis tournaments. Today, tennis is no longer just a leisure activity—it's a serious, high-speed power game. The sport has grown tremendously, and Wimbledon's champions have become global icons. The most important matches are played at the Centre Court,' the guide concluded.

As they stepped toward the legendary Centre Court, the guide pointed to a quote inscribed above the entrance.

It read:

'If you can meet with Triumph and Disaster
And treat those two impostors just the same.'

'That's from Rudyard Kipling's poem "If",' the guide said. 'It reminds every player of the spirit of the game—grace in victory, dignity in defeat.'

The tour ended with a walk through the gift shop. It was filled with souvenirs: towels, racquets, balls, T-shirts, and the traditional strawberries and cream. Ajja picked up a towel with the iconic Wimbledon logo, while Ajji bought a water bottle.

Their schedule was packed, so they couldn't visit Lord's. But Ajja was still thrilled to have seen Wimbledon.

Later that week, Nooni's big day arrived.

Radha's husband, Vijay, also joined them. They reached BVB an hour early to help Nooni get ready. To their surprise, all the students were helping each other. Nooni did *namaskara* to Ajja and Ajji.

They all wished them well.

'Children, be confident, dance well and live your characters. All the best,' Ajja said warmly.

They came out of the green room and took their seats in the auditorium, which filled up quickly.

Radha turned to Ajji and asked, 'Mami, what's so special about Kuchipudi?'

'Kuchipudi is a village in Andhra Pradesh. The dance form gets its name from there. It is one of the eight major Indian classical dance styles. Originally, it was performed only by Brahmin boys—no women were allowed. One of the boys would dress as a woman for female roles. Most of the performances were based on stories of Krishna. But now, women are very much a part of it. Gurus have also started weaving in contemporary themes—nature, the seasons, and more.'

The performance opened with Ganesh Vandana, followed by some stories.

As Nooni was a good dancer, she was given the centre stage.

Each item required a complete change of costume, and the students handled it all brilliantly.

But the standout performance came from a male dancer visiting from Hyderabad. His portrayals of Ishwar, Ram and Krishna were powerful and deeply expressive.

The audience was mesmerized.

At the end of the show, Dr Nandakumar, the director of the Bhavan, came on stage. He praised the troupe's dedication and efforts to showcase the cultural richness of India. Mementoes were distributed to each dancer, followed by warm applause.

Nooni thanked her teacher and took permission to move to Radha's place. In the meantime, Radha took the opportunity to speak with Dr Nandakumar and scheduled a meeting for the next morning.

The very next morning, all of them visited Dr Nandakumar in his office. They narrated the entire story of the lost earrings to him.

After listening carefully, he said, 'Please don't worry. It is always better to make such enquiries through a recognized organization rather than as individuals. We will definitely help you.'

He made quick notes and read them aloud to confirm the details.

A notice was soon drafted and placed on the community bulletin board at the Bhavan. It was also shared via email among other community centres and religious places.

If any family has members named Bharati and Simran Kaur residing in England, we would like to get in touch with you regarding an important matter. Please call this number for further details.

He gave the Bhavan's contact number and informed the receptionist to expect potential enquiries about this.

He assured the family, saying, 'I'm sure people will read this and get back to us. Also, since the names are Bharati and Simran Kaur—and because Kaur suggests a Sikh background—I'll reach out to my friends in the Punjabi and Sikh associations. They have extensive networks and might be able to help us trace them.'

'That is very kind of you,' said Ajji gratefully.

That evening, Radha and her husband, Vijay, treated the family to a West End (Broadway) show titled *The Audience*. The play revolved around Queen Elizabeth II and the many prime ministers she worked with during her long reign. Beginning her role as monarch at the young age of twenty-three, her first prime minister was Winston Churchill. The play traced her transformation—how she grew in stature, carried herself with dignity, offered quiet advice, remained politically neutral, and earned the respect of those around her.

'Please read British history after the play so you will be able to appreciate it more. You'll understand this play even better. It covered only a part of the queen's reign. Remember, the queen met many more prime ministers in her lifetime,' Ajji told Nooni.

Nooni nodded, but her mind was elsewhere. Despite the day's excitement, a worry tugged at her heart. Her mission about the earrings still had no answers.

Threads of the Past

It had been a few days since the notice was shared, and they had not heard from Dr Nandakumar. Nooni began to lose hope.

Then, finally one morning at breakfast time, the phone rang. It was Dr Nandakumar.

'Countless people approached us. My team sifted through the calls and the information they shared,' he said. 'Some were named Simran, and some Bharati—but only one group had both names, and they were sisters. I felt they were genuine because they sounded concerned. Fortunately, both of them are currently in London. Shall we meet them today?'

All of them agreed and went to BVB and waited in a quiet meeting room for the guests to arrive. Ajji's heart was restless. To her, it felt like the final round of an important examination. The earrings had travelled with them from Bangalore to Ujjain, Ujjain to Amritsar, Amritsar to Delhi and finally to London. She prayed that the earrings would return to their rightful owner.

Right on time, four people entered the room.

An old lady in a soft pink phulkari suit led them. She looked frail but walked steadily. By her side was a cheerful, chubby, young girl with short bobbed hair in a smart western outfit. She was perhaps Nooni's age or a little older. Another lady, younger than the older woman and dressed in a long, flowing skirt, followed behind. The last to enter was a tall, middle-aged man in jeans and a T-shirt.

They all sat down opposite the family. Then, slowly, the older woman began to speak.

'This is my sister Bharati Kaur. This is her son, Gobind. That's his daughter Dimple—we call her Bubbly, and I am Simran Kaur. We live in Southampton.'

Ajja introduced himself, Ajji, Nooni and Radha in turn. Dr Nandakumar introduced himself, too, and offered a few warm words.

Then Ajja asked in a concerned tone, 'Is Southampton very far?'

'Not really, it's just about an hour's drive. We have a big Indian community there and even a mandir. Yesterday morning, I saw a notice in the mandir complex about an announcement from Dr Nandakumar, and it made me very curious. So I asked Gobind to call the number on the notice, and he arranged for us to meet today,' replied the older woman.

They all nodded.

'Aunty ji, did you lose anything precious recently at the Bangalore airport?' Nooni asked Simran softly.

With tears welling in her eyes, Simran nodded. 'Yes, it was something very precious and very dear to my heart.'

'What was that?' asked Ajja gently.

'A pair of emerald-green earrings with a peacock design. On the back screw, there's an inscription in Gurmukhi. I lost them during my return from Bangalore to London.'

As she spoke, a few tears escaped down her cheeks. She took a breath and continued.

'I remember the exact date of our travel. When I came to India, I knew in my heart that it would be my last visit. I wanted to meet all my people— my childhood friends, my cousins, my roots. I'm growing old. Gobind was worried about me travelling alone, so he arranged for a caretaker named Sheela to accompany me. Sheela is of Indian origin but had never been to India before. She was excited about the journey.

'We reached Delhi and visited many friends and family. From there, we travelled to Amritsar. I wanted to go to the Harmandir Sahib. While we were there, I got the earrings polished. I also met our old landlord. Afterwards, we went to Bangalore to meet more relatives.

'When we were returning to London, at the Bangalore airport, I opened my purse to tip the porter. The purse had a special compartment where I kept a small pouch with the earrings. While pulling out the money, the pouch nearly fell. I got worried and handed it over to Sheela. I told her to keep it safely in her backpack.

'After that, we went to the restroom. When I came out, I asked Sheela again if she had kept the pouch safely. She said yes, she had put it inside her backpack while we were inside the restroom.

'We checked our luggage in, passed through immigration and then stopped at the food court. It was a bit crowded, but we managed to find a corner to sit. I suggested we have some tea and snacks—one last taste of Indian food before we left. We had tea, some biscuits and a samosa. When the bill came, Sheela offered to pay and pulled some money out of the same backpack.

'We proceeded to the gate and boarded the plane. During the flight, I again asked her about the pouch. She assured me that it was in her cabin baggage, safely stored.

'Once we landed at Heathrow and got home, I was exhausted and went straight to bed. The next day was Bubbly's birthday, and Sheela stayed on to help us prepare. It was hectic, but even in the middle of everything, I remembered the earrings. They were supposed to be Bubbly's birthday gift.

'I called Sheela and asked for the jewellery pouch. We opened the backpack and searched thoroughly. It wasn't there.

'Sheela looked puzzled. She searched again and again. "Aunty ji," she said. "I definitely put it in here."

'I felt a chill run through me. I'm usually calm; I hardly ever lose my temper. But that day, I was furious. "Where did you put it?" I asked. "In the outer zip or the inner one?" Sheela looked lost. She said she couldn't remember. She was sure she had kept it, but couldn't recall exactly where.

'I kept asking her, "Did you leave the pouch in the washroom, on one of the shelves, assuming that you had already put it in your bag? Or did you accidentally slip it into another similar-looking bag? Maybe it fell out when you were paying the bill or removing your passport for verification?" The more I questioned her, the more confused she became. Eventually, she started crying.

'Just then, Gobind came in. "Masi ji, why are you so upset?" he asked.

'I told him, "I've lost a very precious pair of earrings."

'Gobind was surprised. "Earrings? I've never seen you wearing anything special."

'"I never wore them," I said quietly. "They were meant for Bubbly. It was to be my special gift for her sixteenth birthday."

'He sent Sheela out of the room and came to sit beside me.

'"Masi ji," he said gently, "these kids are super sensitive. Let's not make a big deal of it. How much were the earrings worth? Five hundred pounds? A thousand?"

'He put his hand on my shoulder affectionately. "For the sake of a thousand pounds, let's not lose our peace of mind. Let the girl go happily. What's lost is lost. In business, we take losses and move on. I'll count this as one of my business losses," he said.

'I broke down, crying.

'Seeing my tears, Gobind tried to comfort me. "Masi ji, don't cry. If you want to give Bubbly some nice Indian earrings for the celebration tomorrow, let's drive to Leicester. It's just like Delhi or Lahore. There are plenty of jewellery shops with good-quality pieces. They may be a little expensive, but Rab has been kind to us."

'I sobbed and sobbed, trying to come to terms with what had happened. I told myself I wasn't destined to have either pair of earrings. But those weren't just any earrings one could buy in a shop in Leicester. They held the smell of my land . . . the memory of my childhood . . . a parting gift . . . a token of the past . . . and, most importantly, they had been made during the reign of Maharaja Ranjit Singh. They were a family heirloom. No amount of money could replace them.

'I didn't want to ruin Bubbly's birthday. I didn't want anyone to see my sadness. So I smiled on the outside and cried on the inside. I had no enthusiasm to shop for new earrings. Instead, I gave Bubbly a thousand pounds from my pension and said, "Beta, buy something you love—something you can wear on special occasions."'

She paused and took a sip of water, trying to compose herself. But it was hard. Her thoughts kept returning to that painful day.

'I kept thinking,' she continued, 'if only I had known exactly where I lost them, I could have filed a complaint with the lost and found. But I wasn't sure. Was it at the airport? Was it somewhere between checking in and boarding the plane? I cursed myself. "Why did I take them for polishing?" I thought. "I should've waited and done it in Leicester."

'But it was too late. Nothing was in my control.

'I've gone through many difficult times in life. But this . . . this broke me. Those earrings were extremely important to me, and I had protected them all my life. And now . . . I had lost them.

'We tried retracing our steps. All the way from tipping the porter at the Bangalore airport to landing in Heathrow, but I could not recall where I lost them.

'Most probably,' Simran said slowly, 'Sheela must have seen another bag exactly like ours on the restroom rack and, by mistake, put the jewellery pouch into that one. Since it didn't happen inside the plane, it must have happened there — in the restroom.'

Nooni, Ajja and Ajji looked at one another. They were convinced. And above all, they were relieved and happy.

Simran continued, 'I can even describe the pouch. It was a red velvet pouch. It had "Khurana Jewellers" embroidered on it. It was very soft.'

Without a word, Ajji opened her purse and handed over the small red velvet pouch to Simran.

Simran clutched the pouch, her fingers trembling. Her eyes welled up with tears. Then, softly, she whispered, 'Zainab, I love you. It is because of you that I have got this back.'

Everyone was surprised by Simran's reaction.

Gobind walked over. He hugged her and said, 'Masi ji, don't cry. You have found your earrings. But who is Zainab? You have never spoken about her before.'

Simran wiped her tears and looked at the familiar red velvet pouch resting in her lap.

She softly said, 'Beta, that is a long story.'

The Magic of the Lost Earrings

'Prakash Singh and Ansari Beig were famous names in our village, Sultanpur, near what is today the India–Pakistan border,' Simran began, her voice steady.

'There were two large *havelis* in the village that everyone knew—one belonged to the Singh family and the other to the Beig family. They were grand houses, side by side, and both families were respected in the village. I was from the Prakash Singh house, and my closest friend, Zainab, was from the Ansari Beig family. We were around ten years old. For generations, our families had lived like friends, deeply bonded by mutual respect.

'We owned vast pieces of land, herds of horses, cows and buffaloes. Everything we needed was available; women never had to step out to fetch anything. We had a large household, with many helping hands.

'Our fathers and uncles would ride out to the fields on horseback to inspect the crops and return with plenty of fresh vegetables. My grandmother would keep what we needed, and the rest would be distributed freely to the neighbours. We made large quantities of butter and buttermilk at home, and anyone passing by was always welcome to a glass of chaach. It was just how life was—it was unthinkable to charge money for such things.

'It was believed that our ancestors had served in the court of Maharaja Ranjit Singh ji. They were brave soldiers who had fought all the way to Afghanistan. In return for their service, the Maharaja generously rewarded them with acres of fertile land. That land sustained us for generations. But more than the wealth, it was the spirit of sharing that defined our families.

'Every evening, we had music *jalsas* at home. When I look back, I feel as though we lived in a slice of paradise. And along with the land came beautiful ornaments that were gifted to our families

in gratitude. Among them were the earrings — large, green, peacock-shaped, with delicate work in Gurmukhi on the back screws.

'Both my grandmother and Zainab's had a similar pair. When we were little, they passed those earrings down to us — Zainab's were green and mine were red. But they were far too heavy for our ears back then, so we kept them safely locked away. Sometimes, we'd take them out and admire them in secret.

'The women in our families were skilled in embroidery. They had leisure, and they used it creatively. Rashida Begum, Zainab's mother, once embroidered a sari for my mother. In return, my mother made her a baagh dupatta. During Eid, they would send over platters of sweets made with ghee, and we would send back baskets of fresh fruit from our orchard. There was no formality. Just love.'

She paused, holding the velvet pouch gently, as though it contained not just earrings, but the weight of a time that once was.

'But things didn't remain the same,' Simran continued.

'I remember there was a strange, uneasy silence starting to grow in our home. The elders would whisper in hushed tones. "It seems India will be divided," they'd say. "Muslims on one side, Hindus on the other." Someone would ask, "What about the Sikhs?" And the answer would always be vague: "Probably with the Hindus . . . but it's not clear." Some dismissed it as a rumour. "How can our country be divided like this? How can they displace people?" they'd argue. But the whispering didn't stop.

'Gradually, everything changed. The warmth between families like ours and Zainab's turned into tension. There was a strange caution in every interaction. Our homes, once open to each other without thought, now felt closed.

'Then, one day, it happened. An unknown man—someone we'd never seen, never heard of—drew a line through the heart of undivided India. A line. And just like that, everything changed. The line ran through Punjab. And the message was clear: from this moment, this side is one country, and that side another. We were told we had to leave. Our home was no longer ours.

'That line of separation—the Radcliffe Line they later called it—was cruel. It didn't just divide land. It split hearts, families, childhoods and entire lives. My family had lived in Sultanpur for generations. We didn't know any other place.

At most, we visited Karachi, where we had some relatives. Now we had to find a new life in a land we'd never known.

'The men in the house were tense. Ours was a large joint family. The women wept silently. The children, like me, were baffled and frightened.

One night, my mother woke me up urgently. "We're leaving," she whispered. "Right now."

'That moment is etched in my memory. The house was in chaos. Women were searching for their ornaments. The men were hurriedly collecting cash, papers and even pistols. We children were trying to gather our toys. I opened my small drawer, took out the red peacock earrings and tied them tightly into my dupatta. I didn't want to leave them behind.

'My grandfather was shouting instructions: "We'll disperse to different cities in the new country. It's the only way to survive." My mother was pregnant at the time. She was terrified about travelling in that condition. My dada ji looked at her and said, "There's no other way. You cannot give birth here. Even our friends are no longer our friends. Somehow, hold on until we reach a safe place."

'My mother was in deep trouble. But what could she do? Every moment she prayed with desperation. As we passed a small gurdwara, she folded her hands and said, "Let me pass this test, Wahe Guru. If it is a boy, I will name him Gobind." She said it aloud and then sobbed quietly.

'You know, in Punjab, everyone visits gurdwaras, not only Sikhs. We used to go to both the temple and the gurdwara. That night, we walked some distance and then got on a crowded bus. And we walked again. Somehow, after hours of fear and uncertainty, we reached the line. The visible line of separation. We stepped across into an unknown land—this new country that we were told was now our future called India. Bharat.

'I don't know how miracles happen, but one did happen that day. Just after crossing the border, my mother started experiencing labour pains. People were moving in huge groups—children crying, buses overloaded, animals and people packed together, dust rising everywhere. It was one of the most horrible sights I've seen in my life.

'In that chaos, my father noticed a small mud house at the edge of a field. He held my mother's hand and rushed to it. A poor farmer stood outside the house. When he saw my mother's condition, he welcomed us without a second thought. There was a small cowshed beside the house, and my mother gave birth right there in the cowshed. The farmer's wife helped her.

'My sister was born on Indian soil. She became the first in our family to be an Indian citizen by birth. My mother named her Bharati.'

There was complete silence in the room. It was as if, through Simran, they were transported back in time to witness one of the darkest periods in Indian history.

'What happened to Zainab?' asked Nooni, as she gently walked across and held Simran's hand.

Simran smiled sadly. 'That night, just as we were leaving, Zainab somehow came to know. In the darkness, she ran to me. Without letting anyone notice, she whispered "Insha Allah" in my ear and quickly tied something to the end of my dupatta. She turned to run, but I stopped her.

'I had nothing with me. All our jewellery was packed and locked away. I wanted to give her something in return. That's when I remembered the ring on my finger—a simple one with a red stone. It was the only ornament I had on me. I immediately removed it and gave it to her. "Take this," I said. "This is my gift to you." And then, in the darkness, we disappeared into two different worlds.'

There was silence in the room. No one wanted to interrupt Simran's thoughts.

She finally continued, 'When we came to India, I realized that my dada ji had already started selling our family jewellery bit by bit to provide for us. He did it with tears in his eyes, and with a heavy heart. My grandmother, though, was full of hope. She believed that one day, we would go back and reclaim our home.

'She would argue, "I've locked the house in three places. I've left the lights on so people think we're still living there. No one will touch our home." But little did she know. People could break the lock. They could ransack the house. They could take everything.'

Simran paused, her hands folded in her lap. Her eyes were filled with both pain and peace. 'I lost my home. But I never lost Zainab. She gave me something to hold on to—and now, Wahe Guru has given it back to me.

'The day I untied the knot in my dupatta, I discovered two precious gifts. On one end were the red-studded earrings given to me by my grandmother, and on the other, Zainab's green-studded earrings. By then, I knew that if the elders in the family found out I had any jewellery, they would sell or mortgage it. So I never told anyone.

It became my secret—two beautiful, delicate memories of the life I had left behind.

'After Partition, our family was scattered across different places. But the truth was, the men in our family didn't have any skills. For generations, they had lived like zamindars, raised in comfort and privilege. The women had never imagined a life where they would have to work for survival.

'But in India, we realized very quickly that land titles could not be transferred. We had to start from nothing. Some of the younger ones adapted. They took up small jobs, started businesses and worked very hard. But for the older generation, it was devastating. Their pride wouldn't allow them to take on work that would earn them a living. Their self-worth was tied to status, not survival.

'My father became a supervisor at a gurdwara in Amritsar and, later, a salaried manager. My mother, who had once embroidered just to pass the time, now did that same work for others for money. For them, it was punishment. They aged rapidly. Their world shrank. They kept reminiscing about the old days and slowly withdrew from life around them.

'I became a mother to Bharati. She was much younger, and both my parents were often too lost in their sorrow to care for her properly. I bathed her, fed her and marked every milestone of her early life. I learnt to cook and took her along when I went to school. After after my matriculation, I didn't go to college. I took up a teaching job instead to support our home. I gave tuition in the evenings to earn a little more.

'When I reached marriageable age, my parents were torn. They still lived in the illusion that they would find a match befitting their former status. But I knew better. I pushed those thoughts aside. I couldn't afford to think of marriage. If I had married and moved away, Bharati would have been forced to leave school and take up some small job to help support the family. I couldn't let that happen.'

There was a soft sob from behind Simran. Bharati, who had been listening quietly, was now wiping her eyes.

Simran turned slightly and said, 'I don't know why I'm speaking about all this today. I never talk about the past. I'm not like our parents. They held on to everything—their land, their titles, their memories. But it made them bitter. It made them old.

'Bharati was different. When she got a first class in her matriculation, she told me she wanted to study medicine. But we just didn't have the means. She understood. Instead, she chose nursing, which was a shorter course, so that she could start working by the age of twenty. She studied well, with full focus. With the help of my landlord's daughter, Daman Kaur, I sold the red pair to Kewal Ram and used that money to support Bharati's education.

'Soon, she met a pharmacy student, also a refugee like us, and I supported them. Since he didn't have a home of his own, he stayed with us. They had a child. My mother had always wanted a boy in the family to be named after the tenth Sikh Guru—Gobind Singh ji. By then, our parents were no longer with us. But I remembered her wish and told Bharati.'

'Sikh Guru Gobind Singh is very famous. To protect the helpless pandits of Kashmir, he fought the Mughals and martyred his four sons—two teenagers and two young children, aged six and eight,' Ajji said.

Gobind looked at his Masi with affection.

'Bharati had earned a reputation as a kind and capable nurse, though her salary was modest. One day, she saw an advertisement for Indian nurses in Aberdeen and asked, "Didi, should I apply? It could help us financially, but it would mean leaving Gobind and my husband behind." It's a big sacrifice for a mother.'

Simran looked at Bharati with loving eyes.

Bharati said, 'Those were the hardest days of my life. I realized nothing in this world comes free—except a sister's love. With Didi's blessings and my husband's support, I decided to go. I had never been on a plane, only seen planes in the sky. But I boarded one in Delhi and flew to London, determined to give my son a better future.

'Back then, there were very few Indians here—mostly elite professionals in Oxford or Cambridge. Nurses were rare. Winters were bitter. I'd cry, wanting to return home. Phone calls were unaffordable, and letters took months. Still, I had made up my mind to stay. I saved every penny of my first salary, even walked to work to avoid spending on the bus. In eighteen months, I had saved enough to bring my family here. The visa process was simpler then. When Gobind was three, he didn't even recognize me. That broke my heart. But I consoled myself: he had Didi, and *masi* is nothing but *maa jaisi*, like mother.

'We were given a city government house. Didi took up babysitting work as she couldn't teach here without training. My husband worked as a delivery boy at a nearby pharmacy. Later, both of them cleared their exams. My husband became a locum pharmacist, and Didi began teaching again. Eventually, we bought our own house.

'Didi wanted to live separately, but I said, "You're my mother. I won't let you live alone." Since I didn't become a doctor, I specialized as an OT nurse. Gobind became a pharmacist and started his own store,' Bharati concluded.

A deep silence followed. Even the ever-chatty Ajji found no words. It felt as though time stood still, as if one end of the pendulum had swung back to Partition.

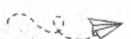

Finally, the time to say goodbye came. Everyone was moved to tears by the story of love, loss and the resilience of immigrants.

'We're truly grateful to Nooni and her grandparents for searching for us across cities and countries. God has been kind. May I at least pay for your travel expenses?' Gobind said.

Ajja and Ajji immediately said, 'No, we would have come to London even otherwise. It's just a happy coincidence that we happened

to visit the very places connected to your past. Dr Nandakumar was very helpful in tracing you all. There were many people who helped us in returning these earrings to you—the old man at Khurana Jewellers, who gave us Kewal Ram's address; Amrit Ram, who told us about Daman Kaur, she guided us to Mary D'Souza, who led us to London; and the curator in Delhi, who helped us with the exhibition details.'

Ajja, looking around the room, felt as though they were all part of a big family. He said, 'If you are all willing, shall we go and see the exhibition tomorrow since it is the opening day?'

Bharati immediately agreed. 'Of course! Please let us buy the tickets for everyone.'

Simran turned to Gobind and said, 'Beta, as per Sikh tradition, we must invite our guests home for a meal before they leave. Kindly fix up a date and the time.'

She then turned towards Bubbly and said, 'Bubbly, Nooni is your age. Take her to some interesting place, somewhere both of you can enjoy.'

Turning to Ajji, Simran added, 'Bubbly knows every nook and corner of London.'

Simran took out the earrings from the pouch, held them up to the light and said, 'Bubbly, look at this—the peacocks are dancing with happiness. Though late, happy birthday, beta.' She handed over the earrings to her granddaughter.

Bubbly's eyes welled up. She immediately hugged her Dadi and asked, 'Dadi, where is Zainab now? The way Nooni found us, maybe we can also find Zainab?'

Gobind, who realized Simran was too overwhelmed after having relived her past, said, 'Yes, beta. Once we get home, we'll definitely try.'

Full Circle

Bright and early the next morning, they headed to the Victoria and Albert Museum.

Everybody was keen to explore the museum in their own way. For Simran, it was deeply personal — her earrings, once part of her childhood, had become a national treasure and were now on display in a foreign land. For Ajji, it was like a sweet shop for a child with a sweet tooth. She wanted to see every object related to India's history. For Ajja, it was the building itself — its architecture. Radha had visited many times and didn't feel the same excitement but was happy to accompany the others.

They joined one of the hourly free guided tours.

The guide said, 'You require several days to see the V&A Museum. It depends on your interests.

We house a unique collection of objects of historical significance, artistic brilliance and scientific curiosity from across the world.'

As they entered, they saw a stunning collection of royal costumes, once worn by kings and queens, still preserved in all their splendour. Then, on the left, they noticed a small object displayed in a glass case. It looked like ten finger rings with curved, sharp edges, accompanied by a short description:

> 'Using these finger rings, Shivaji of the Maratha dynasty killed Afzal Khan of the Adil Shahi court.'

Ajji folded her hands in reverence for King Shivaji. Everybody was surprised.

The guide asked, 'What is this for?'

Ajji said, 'Shivaji was a great warrior and the founder of the Maratha Empire. Though short in stature, Shivaji challenged the mighty Mughals in the north and the Adil Shahi rulers in the south. Afzal Khan, a towering man over seven feet tall, was sent to assassinate him. Shivaji, knowing this, wore these rings hidden under his gloves. When Afzal Khan tried to strangle him during a supposed embrace, Shivaji struck first—he punched him with these claws. In India, we consider Shivaji a national hero. He's remembered for his bravery and for protecting Indian culture. He is known as the pride of Maharashtra and India.'

Nooni and Ajja looked at each other and smiled. They knew Ajji was in her element.

The group continued to the next section, which displayed exquisite artefacts and artworks. Among them were pencil sketches by Leonardo da Vinci.

'Leonardo,' the guide said, 'was an Italian artist and inventor, best known for painting the *Mona Lisa*, which now hangs in the Louvre Museum in Paris. Though the painting itself seems simple, the mysterious smile of the woman in it has fascinated people for centuries. The artist studied human anatomy in detail and made numerous sketches before creating a final work. What you see here are those preparatory sketches—each drawing a study in precision and imagination.'

They then moved to the royal gift section. During Queen Victoria's reign as Empress of India, many Indian kings, nawabs and sultans sent her lavish gifts. This part of the museum displayed those offerings crafted in gold, silver, ivory, rubies, diamonds and wood. The guide pointed to an intricately carved wooden box.

'This,' he said, 'is made from sandalwood, known for its fragrance and beauty. It was gifted by a king from Karnataka, a state in southern India famous for sandalwood, fine silk and exquisite craftsmanship.'

Nooni immediately said, 'We are from there, and we are very proud of our heritage. We have great artists who have created masterpieces in stone—we call them poetry in stone.'

Everyone clapped. Nooni beamed with pride.

They then moved to the next exhibit. The guide said, 'All of you are very lucky. We have a special travelling exhibition from India right now. It will be here for two weeks. India is a vast land with many cultures, civilizations and is a heaven for artists.'

He pointed to a long, beautifully lit display. 'Here you'll see earrings from the Mauryan period to the present day. From tribal communities to royal courts, from the forest to the palace, earrings have always been a symbol of identity and artistry. They were made from everything—baked mud, wood, beads, coral, seashells, cowrie shells, silver, gold, diamonds and other precious stones. Please take a walk around and enjoy.'

But Ajji and the others weren't looking at everything. They were searching for a special pair: red stone, peacock-shaped earrings.

'Sir,' Nooni asked the guide, 'do you have any earrings from Maharaja Ranjit Singh's period? We're very keen to see them.'

The guide replied, 'Oh, yes. The second-last section belongs to Maharaja Ranjit Singh's period. I checked it yesterday morning before heading to college.'

Ajja's ears perked up. He asked, 'Are you going to a college?'

The guide said, 'Yes, I'm a professor of history. I love to lead tours because it connects me with people. In the process, I have also visited India. I spent a year studying the Sikh Empire. Maharaja Ranjit Singh was a remarkable ruler with great vision and a lion's heart.'

Ajja nodded in appreciation. Ajji beamed. At last, someone who shared her passion for history.

And then—they found it.

A beam of light reflected off a glass case, casting a soft glow on the earrings inside. They shimmered with a quiet brilliance. It was an exact match to the pair Bubbly was wearing that day.

Everyone's face lit up with joy.

Simran walked up to the glass and gently placed her hand on it. Once, these earrings had been a treasured heirloom of her family. She had never worn them, and yet they carried the weight of her history. They had travelled farther than she ever imagined—crossing borders soaked in sorrow, surviving decades of silence, journey across continents and finally arriving here, preserved in a foreign land.

She gazed at them not only with affection but with reverence. They were no longer mere ornaments—they were memory, they were loss, they were resilience. And then, slowly, she let go of possession, pain and longing with quiet detachment.

After a long tour, as they were leaving, Gobind said, 'Tomorrow, Bubbly will take you around London. Of course, you'd need months to see everything in London—parks, museums, historical places—but since your time is limited, she'll show you a few important places. I have hired a van for the next three days. It is the least we can do for you.'

The next morning, the van arrived at Radha's house. Ajji helped Radha pack lunchboxes for everyone, and they left to see the Tower of London. When they arrived, they were surprised to see the security guards dressed in black-and-red uniforms with distinctive black hats.

Bubbly said, 'Our school brings us here for study tours. These are the costumes worn by royal guards. Every major site here has guided tours, or you can hire headphones with digital codes to learn more. There are also pocket maps available here. All these help tourists to explore and understand the monuments.'

Like most Indian visitors, they were keen to see the Kohinoor diamond. Ajji explained to the guide, 'Kohinoor originated in India. Then it went to Iran and Afghanistan and eventually returned to India before ending up here. Apart from the Kohinoor, there are many beautiful crowns, sceptres and other royal jewels on display.'

A conveyor belt moved slowly past the Crown Jewels, allowing everyone a glimpse without stopping.

The guide explained, 'The Tower of London is deeply tied to British history. It has served as both a fort and a palace. It is built along the river

Thames, and the famous Tower Bridge is nearby. The bridge is painted blue, and there are several poems about it, the most famous being "London Bridge is falling down".'

At the souvenir shops, Ajji bought a couple of fridge magnets shaped like the tower.

From there, they headed to Hyde Park, a vast green expanse in the heart of London.

Bubbly said, 'This is Speakers' Corner. Anyone can give a speech here about anything and anyone, except the royal family.'

She continued, 'The British royal family has been around for nearly a thousand years and is well respected. The monarch lives in Buckingham Palace. At a fixed time each day, there's a ceremony called 'the changing of the guards' which you can attend if you like.'

They sat on the grass and had their lunch.

Ajji reminded everyone, 'We must put all the trash in the bins and leave the place clean.'

Next, they visited Big Ben and the Houses of Parliament.

Bubbly said, 'When we were studying British history at school, our teacher brought us here and explained the roles of the House of Commons and the House of Lords. This hall was once a tennis court used by Henry VIII.' She pointed to a few paintings on the wall. Ajji immediately recognized one.

'That's Jehangir with Thomas Roe,' she said. 'Roe was the first British envoy to visit Jehangir's court and sought permission to trade from the port of Surat. This moment marked the beginning of British involvement in India.'

Since Parliament was not in session, they could enter and view the House of Commons. Ajji added, 'Democracy here evolved gradually. Britain is one of the oldest practising democracies.'

'Ajji, their Parliament building is so small!' said Nooni.

'Yes, because they don't have space to expand,' Ajji replied with a smile.

They crossed the street and walked a short distance to a heavily guarded gate.

'This is our Prime Minister's residence,' Bubbly said. 'It's called 10 Downing Street.'

Ajji asked, 'Can we peep in?'

Bubbly said, 'Due to security reasons, we can't. The prime minister and the finance minister live here, and the rest of the building is used as office space.'

From there, they walked across to the statues opposite the Parliament building.

Bubbly explained, 'These are the world leaders who have made significant contributions to global history.'

Ajji started to make notes. There were statues of Nelson Mandela, Mohandas Gandhi, Margaret Thatcher, Clement Attlee, Winston Churchill, Abraham Lincoln and a few more.

Ajji said, 'I would like a photograph with Mahatma Gandhi. In a way, the man who led our freedom struggle stands here, too. It makes me very proud.'

The following day, they visited Madame Tussauds.

Bubbly said, 'Madame Tussaud was a French artist known for her wax sculptures. Today, the museum features life-sized statues of famous people from around the world. It gives the public a chance to see their replicas, especially if they can't meet them in real life.'

India had a strong presence—political leaders such as Narendra Modi, Indira Gandhi and Rajiv Gandhi; film stars such as Shah Rukh Khan, Madhuri Dixit and Amitabh Bachchan; legends like Lata Mangeshkar, Sachin Tendulkar and M.S.

Dhoni. The figures were so lifelike, it was hard to believe they were made of wax.

In the afternoon, Ajji said, 'I'd like to rest at home, especially since we're going for dinner to Simran ji's house.'

Nooni was keen to visit the London Eye. The giant wheel, inaugurated in 2000, is the world's largest cantilevered observation wheel with thirty-two capsules.

Bubbly added, 'Actually, there are only thirty-two, but they've labelled them up to thirty-three because there's no capsule numbered thirteen.'

Nooni laughed. 'Even in this modern, scientific world, people still avoid the number thirteen?'

'Yes, they do,' Bubbly replied. 'But it's still one of London's biggest attractions.'

Luckily, there wasn't a long queue that day. Since it wasn't peak time, they got tickets without much wait.

'If you come in the evening,' Bubbly said, 'you can see the entire city illuminated. The river Thames sparkles, and from the top, you get a panoramic view of London. But in summer, the queues can be very long, especially near sunset.'

That night, they all went to Simran Kaur's residence for dinner. It was a warm, modern house with five bedrooms and a small garden.

When they settled in, Simran said, 'Gobind has done well. He now owns two pharmacies. Once upon a time, his father worked as a delivery boy and later as a locum. Today, Gobind is the owner. I always remind him that if an immigrant comes with a prescription and can't afford some medicines, he should help them out. Remember, we were in their shoes.

Dinner was a delicious spread of typical Punjabi fare—paneer dishes, assorted parathas, a series of savoury courses and rich sweets. As they ate and chatted, Ajji told everyone about Somanahalli, the temple, the stepwell, and the lost family story on the banks of the Tungabhadra River.

When it was time to leave, Simran handed Nooni a small gift box. When she opened it, she gasped. Inside was a pair of elegant, contemporary English gold earrings.

'Why such an expensive gift for Nooni?' asked Ajji.

Simran smiled. 'She is like Bubbly to me. Bubbly lost her earrings and got them back. This is a small way to mark the memory. I'm sure whenever Nooni wears these, she'll remember us and the story of the lost earrings,' said Simran.

Nooni immediately hugged Simran and thanked her.

Simran then said, 'I would like to share some happy news. After hearing your story and the way you searched for us, I felt inspired to search for Zainab. I went to the Pakistani community centre and gave them all the information I had about her. They posted on social media, and believe it or not, they found her. She's living in America, settled there with her children. I got her phone number, and we did a video call.'

Simran's voice trembled. 'When I saw her, I burst into tears, and she, too, cried. Both of us have grown old. We laughed, we cried, we remembered. Her children said they'll bring her to London soon—it's just a six-hour flight from New York. I have invited her to come see the Maharaja Ranjit Singh exhibit and to see the earrings.

'During the video call, I also showed her the earrings she had given me. Zainab showed me the little red-stone ring I had given her. She had kept it safe all these years. Both of us remembered our good old days, laughed and cried. A simple pencil line on a map had divided us. But today, technology brought us back together.'

Ajji nodded with joy. 'Thanks to modern technology! It really can unite people when used properly.'

She turned to Simran's family and said, 'You must come visit us in Somanahalli. Karnataka is a beautiful state. You'll love the temples of Halebidu and Belur, the grandeur of Hampi, the Jog Falls, the Gol Gumbaz in Bijapur and the caves of Badami—so many wonders!'

As they prepared to leave, Ajja joked, 'Nooni, what's your next adventure? In the last few years, you've helped us discover a lost temple, a lost family story and now lost earrings!'

'Ajja,' said Nooni with a smile, 'it's all because of Ajji. She encouraged me to care about history and to keep asking questions until I find the answers.'

Ajji added, 'That's the point of learning history: we must remember the joys of the past so we can carry them forward. And we must remember the mistakes so we don't repeat them.'

Simran turned to Nooni and said, 'My dear child, we are deeply grateful to you. Anyone else in your position would have just kept the earrings and forgotten about the owner. But you travelled

all this way simply to do what was right. May god bless you.'

Nooni smiled at her, a little shy but happy inside. She hadn't expected such warmth, only to return something that didn't belong to her.

Sensing Nooni's quiet pride, Ajji placed a gentle hand on her shoulder and said, 'This is the value we hold close, Nooni: doing the right thing even when it's hard. In our culture, we believe the world is one family. Our ancestors taught us, "Small minds create division, but those with large hearts see the whole world as one family—*Vasudhaiva Kutumbakam.*" And through this journey with the lost earrings, you've truly lived that belief.'

Read More in Puffin

The Magic of the Lost Temple

Sudha Murty

City girl Nooni is surprised at the pace of life in her grandparents' village in Karnataka. But she quickly gets used to the gentle routine there and involves herself in a flurry of activities, including papad making, organizing picnics and learning to ride a cycle with her newfound friends.

Things get exciting when Nooni stumbles upon an ancient, fabled stepwell right in the middle of a forest. Join the intrepid Nooni on an adventure of a lifetime in this much-awaited book by Sudha Murty that is heart-warming, charming and absolutely unputdownable.

Read More in Puffin

The Magic of the Lost Story

Sudha Murty

After staying in the lockdown for over a year, Nooni is now visiting her Ajja-Ajji in Somanahalli. Memories of excavating the famous stepwell and experiencing village life for the first time in The Magic of the Lost Temple are still afresh in Nooni's mind. Excited to finally step out of the confines of her home, little does Nooni know she will make yet another discovery, only this time it's a missing puzzle in her family's history.

Written in India's favourite storyteller's inimitable style, The Magic of the Lost Story captures the value of asking questions and keeping the answers alive. Packed with delightful artworks and wondrous terrains, this story takes you on an unforgettable journey as it follows the magnificent Tungabhadra River.

Scan QR code to access the
Penguin Random House India website